THE FINANCE SMURF

That night, everyone sleeps peacefully in the village... That is, almost everyone...
Z
Z
Z
How much for that sarsaparilla leaf?
Three smurfs!
The next day...
Thanks, Sculptor Smurf, it's exactly what I was smurfing for!
CLAY
Careful, Handy Smurf, don't smurf any on the side!

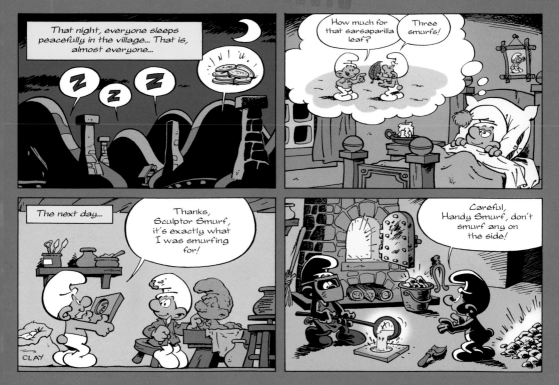

A SMURFS GRAPHIC NOVEL BY PEYO

WITH THE COLLABORATION OF
THIERRY CULLIFORD FOR THE SCRIPT,
ALAIN MAURY AND LUC PARTHOENS FOR ARTWORK,
NINE AND STUDIO LÉONARDO FOR COLORS.

PAPERCUTZ™
NEW YORK

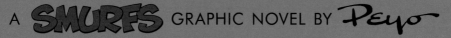

SMURFS GRAPHIC NOVELS AVAILABLE FROM PAPERCUTZ™

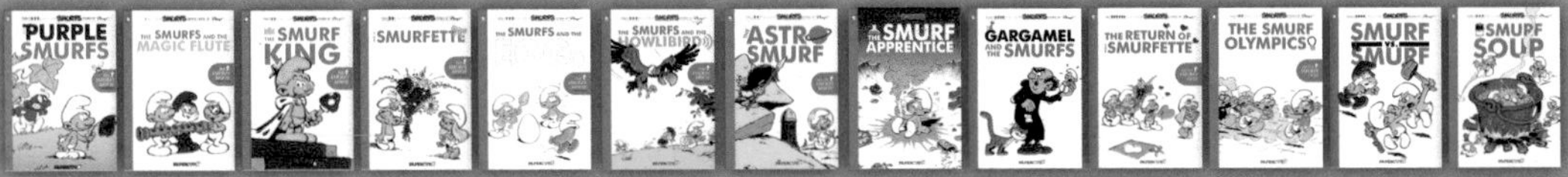
PURPLE SMURFS
THE SMURFS AND THE MAGIC FLUTE
THE SMURF KING
SMURFETTE
THE SMURFS AND THE HOWLIBIRD
ASTRO SMURF
SMURF APPRENTICE
GARGAMEL AND THE SMURFS
THE RETURN OF THE SMURFETTE
THE SMURF OLYMPICS
SMURF VS SMURF
SMURF SOUP

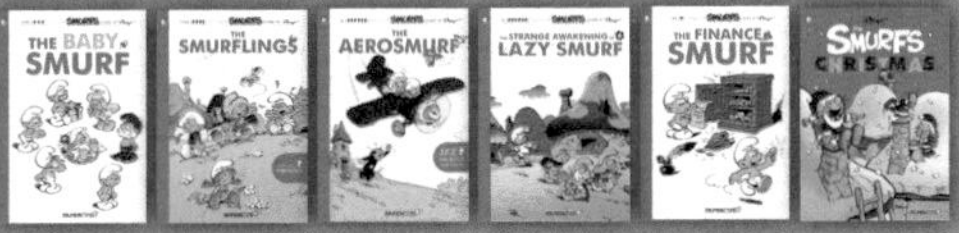
THE BABY SMURF
THE SMURFLINGS
THE AEROSMURF
LAZY SMURF
THE FINANCE SMURF

1. **THE PURPLE SMURFS**
2. **THE SMURFS AND THE MAGIC FLUTE**
3. **THE SMURF KING**
4. **THE SMURFETTE**
5. **THE SMURFS AND THE EGG**
6. **THE SMURFS AND THE HOWLIBIRD**
7. **THE ASTROSMURF**
8. **THE SMURF APPRENTICE**
9. **GARGAMEL AND THE SMURFS**
10. **THE RETURN OF THE SMURFETTE**
11. **THE SMURF OLYMPICS**
12. **SMURF VS. SMURF**
13. **SMURF SOUP**
14. **THE BABY SMURF**
15. **THE SMURFLINGS**
16. **THE AEROSMURF**
17. **THE STRANGE AWAKENING OF LAZY SMURF**
18. **THE FINANCE SMURF**

- THE SMURF CHRISTMAS

COMING SOON:

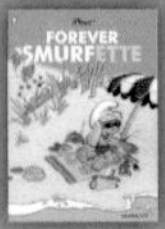
FOREVER SMURFETTE

- FOREVER SMURFETTE

THE SMURFS graphic novels are available in paperback for $5.99 each and in hardcover for $10.99 each at booksellers everywhere. You can also order online at papercutz.com. Or call 1-800-886-1223, Monday through Friday, 9 – 5 EST. MC, Visa, and AmEx accepted. To order by mail, please add $4.00 for postage and handling for first book ordered, $1.00 for each additional book and make check payable to NBM Publishing. Send to: Papercutz, 160 Broadway, Suite 700, East Wing, New York, NY 10038.

THE SMURFS graphic novels are also available digitally wherever e-books are sold.

PAPERCUTZ.COM

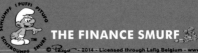

THE FINANCE SMURF

"The Finance Smurf"
BY PEYO
WITH THE COLLABORATION OF
THIERRY CULLIFORD FOR THE SCRIPT,
ALAIN MAURY AND LUC PARTHOENS FOR ARTWORK,
NINE AND STUDIO LÉONARDO FOR COLORS.

Joe Johnson, *SMURFLATIONS*
Adam Grano, *SMURFIC DESIGN*
Janice Chiang, *LETTERING SMURFETTE*
Matt. Murray, *SMURF CONSULTANT*
Beth Scorzato, *SMURF COORDINATOR*
Michael Petranek, *ASSOCIATE SMURF*
Jim Salicrup, *SMURF-IN-CHIEF*

PAPERBACK EDITION ISBN: 978-1-59707-724-8
HARDCOVER EDITION ISBN: 978-1-59707-725-5

PRINTED IN CHINA JULY 2014 BY WKT CO. LTD.
3/F PHASE I LEADER INDUSTRIAL CENTRE
188 TEXACO ROAD, TSEUN WAN, N.T., HONG KONG

Papercutz books may be purchased for business or promotional use. For information on bulk purchases please contact Macmillan Corporate and Premium Sales Department at (800) 221-7945 x5442.

DISTRIBUTED BY MACMILLAN
FIRST PAPERCUTZ PRINTING

THE FINANCE SMURF

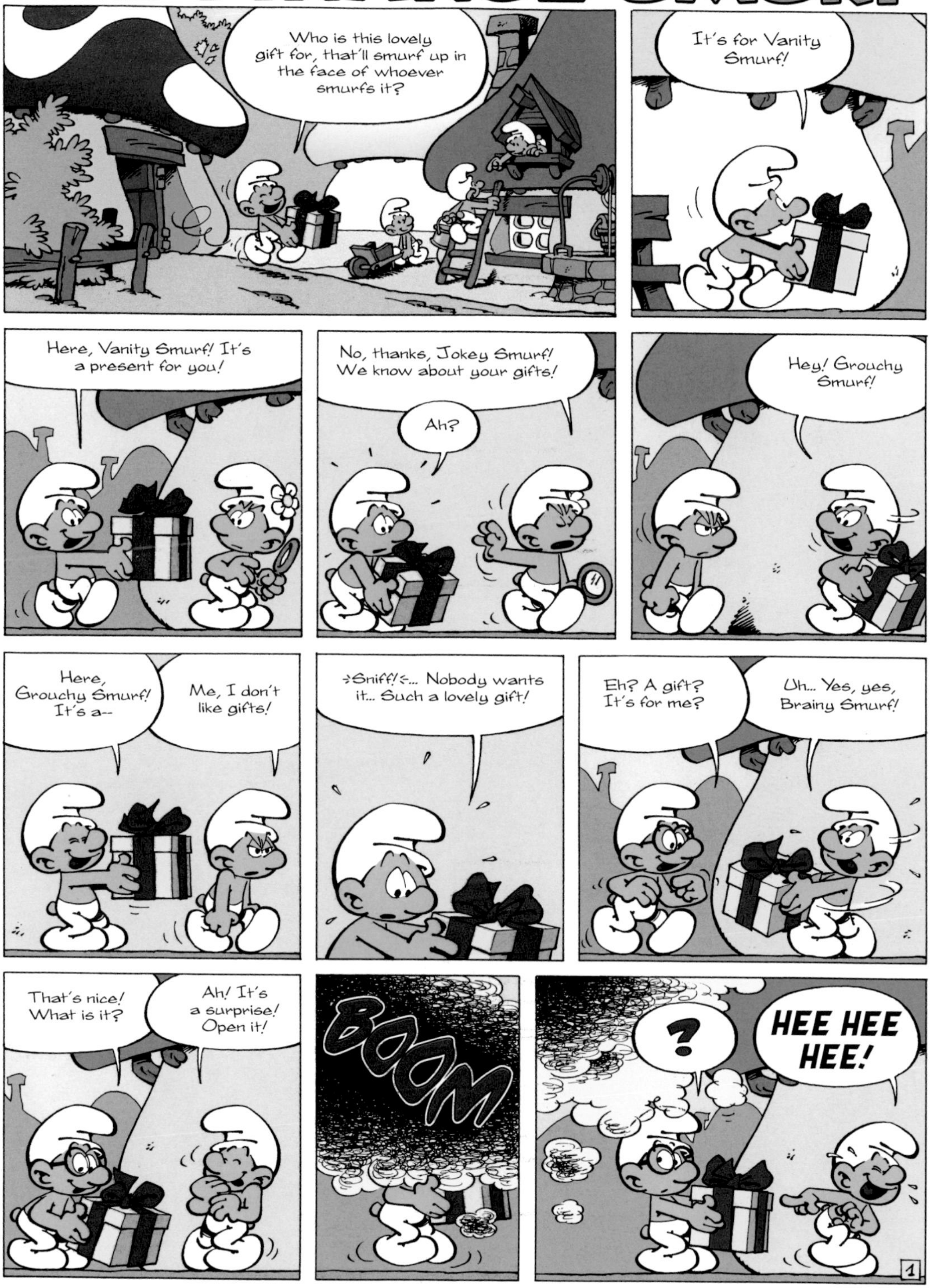
Who is this lovely gift for, that'll smurf up in the face of whoever smurfs it?
It's for Vanity Smurf!
Here, Vanity Smurf! It's a present for you!
No, thanks, Jokey Smurf! We know about your gifts!
Ah?
Hey! Grouchy Smurf!
Here, Grouchy Smurf! It's a--
Me, I don't like gifts!
>Sniff!<... Nobody wants it... Such a lovely gift!
Eh? A gift? It's for me?
Uh... Yes, yes, Brainy Smurf!
That's nice! What is it?
Ah! It's a surprise! Open it!
BOOM
?
HEE HEE HEE!
1

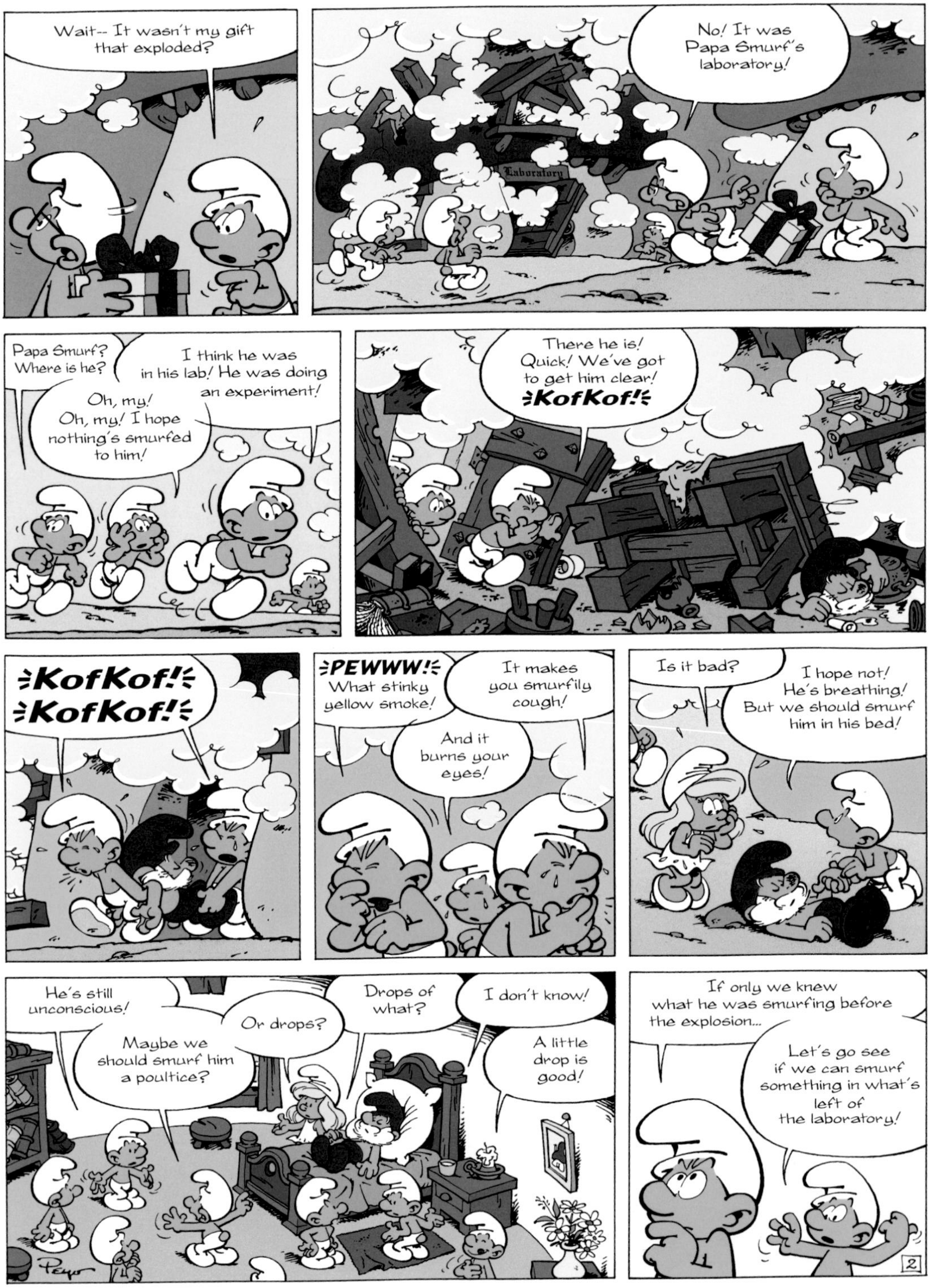
Wait-- It wasn't my gift that exploded?
No! It was Papa Smurf's laboratory!
Laboratory
Papa Smurf? Where is he?
I think he was in his lab! He was doing an experiment!
Oh, my! Oh, my! I hope nothing's smurfed to him!
There he is! Quick! We've got to get him clear! KofKof!
KofKof! KofKof!
PEWWW! What stinky yellow smoke!
It makes you smurfily cough!
And it burns your eyes!
Is it bad?
I hope not! He's breathing! But we should smurf him in his bed!
He's still unconscious!
Maybe we should smurf him a poultice?
Or drops?
Drops of what?
I don't know!
A little drop is good!
If only we knew what he was smurfing before the explosion...
Let's go see if we can smurf something in what's left of the laboratory!
2

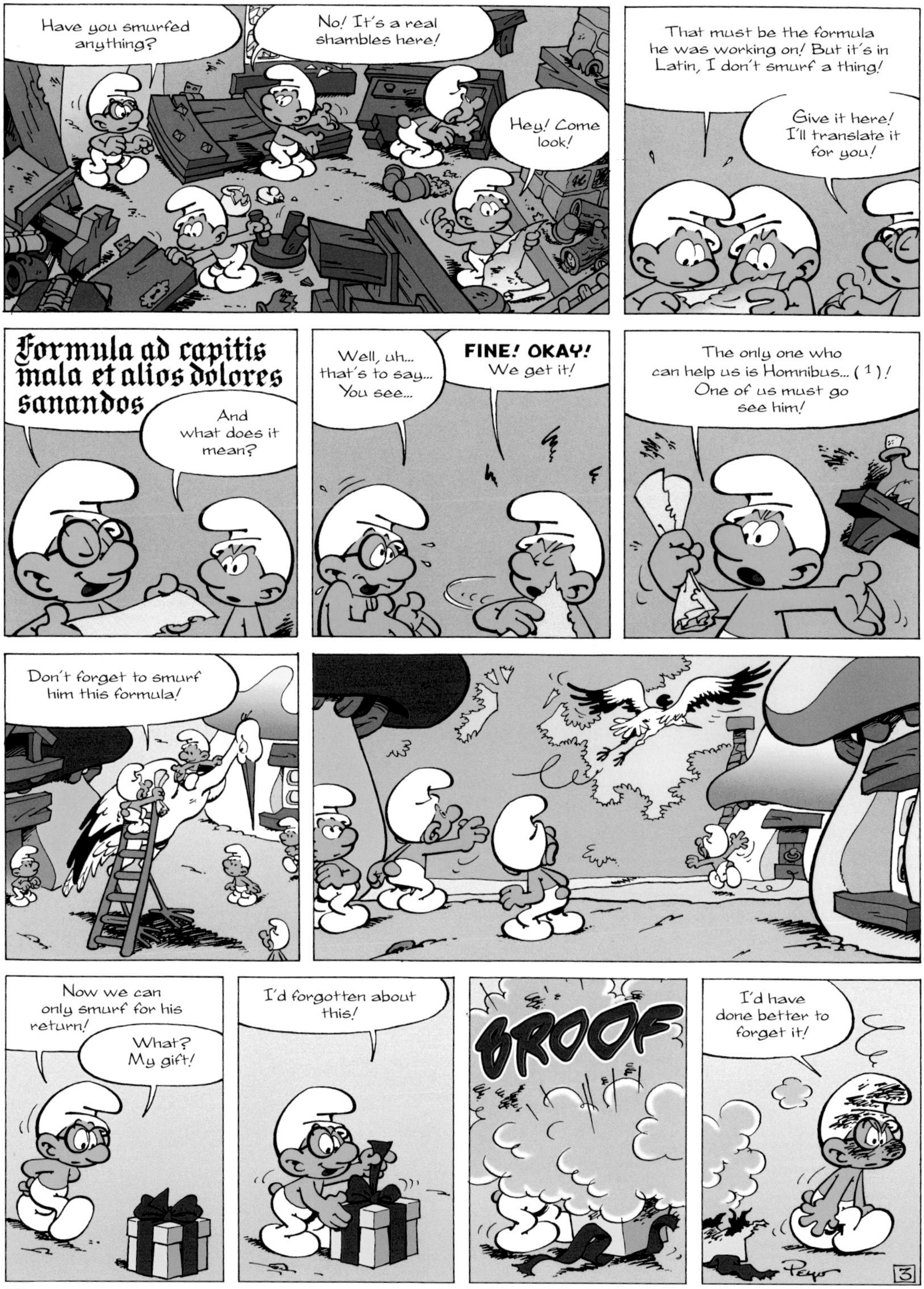

Have you smurfed anything?
No! It's a real shambles here!
Hey! Come look!
That must be the formula he was working on! But it's in Latin, I don't smurf a thing!
Give it here! I'll translate it for you!
Formula ad capitis mala et alios dolores sanandos
And what does it mean?
Well, uh... that's to say... You see...
FINE! OKAY! We get it!
The only one who can help us is Homnibus... (1)! One of us must go see him!
Don't forget to smurf him this formula!
Now we can only smurf for his return!
What? My gift!
I'd forgotten about this!
BROOF
I'd have done better to forget it!
Peyo
3

(1) Homnibus, the good wizard, was last seen in THE SMURFS #2 "The Smurfs and the Magic Flute."

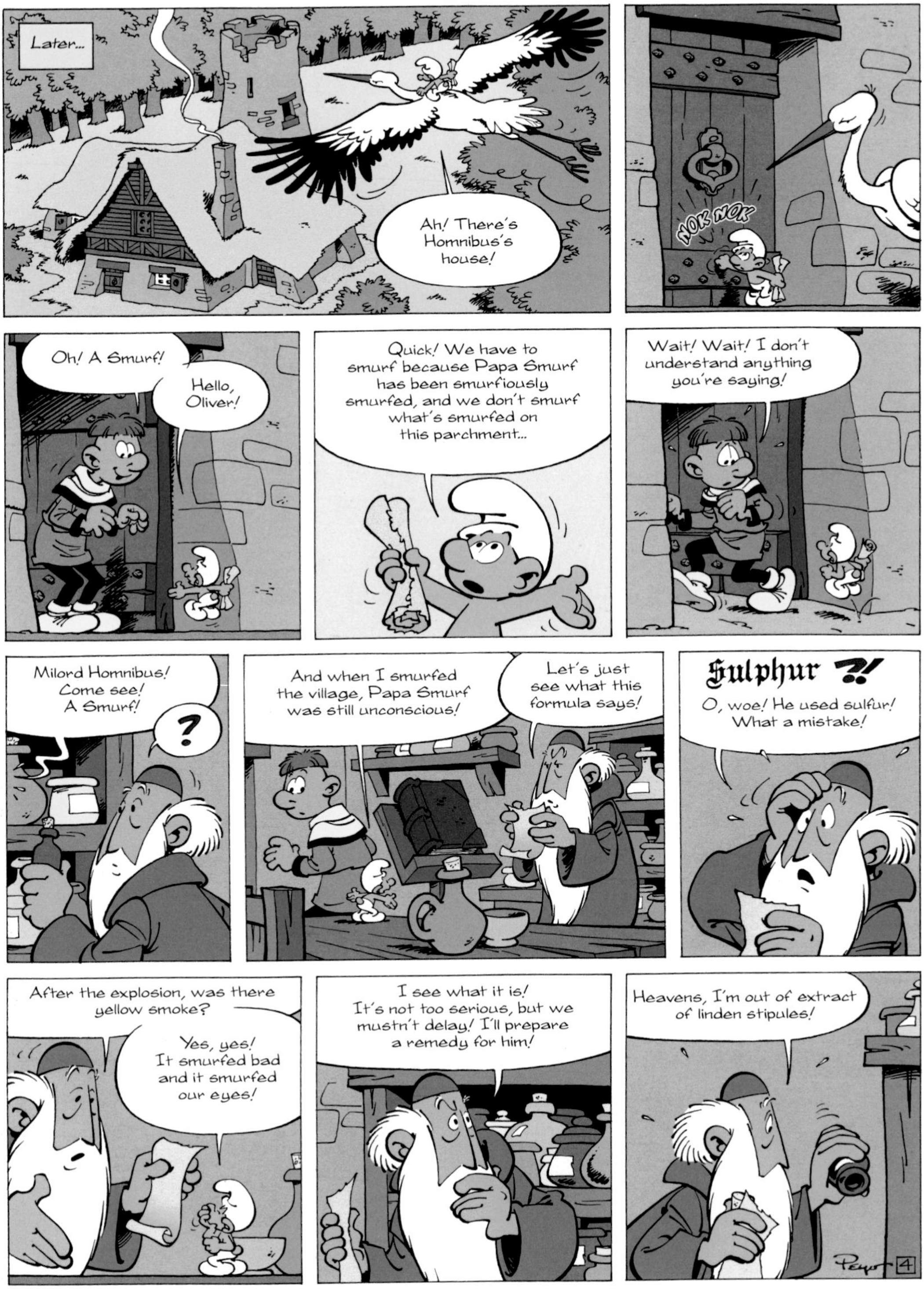
Later...
Ah! There's Homnibus's house!
NOK NOK
Oh! A Smurf!
Hello, Oliver!
Quick! We have to smurf because Papa Smurf has been smurfiously smurfed, and we don't smurf what's smurfed on this parchment...
Wait! Wait! I don't understand anything you're saying!
Milord Homnibus! Come see! A Smurf!
?
And when I smurfed the village, Papa Smurf was still unconscious!
Let's just see what this formula says!
Sulphur ?!
O, woe! He used sulfur! What a mistake!
After the explosion, was there yellow smoke?
Yes, yes! It smurfed bad and it smurfed our eyes!
I see what it is! It's not too serious, but we mustn't delay! I'll prepare a remedy for him!
Heavens, I'm out of extract of linden stipules!
Peyo 4

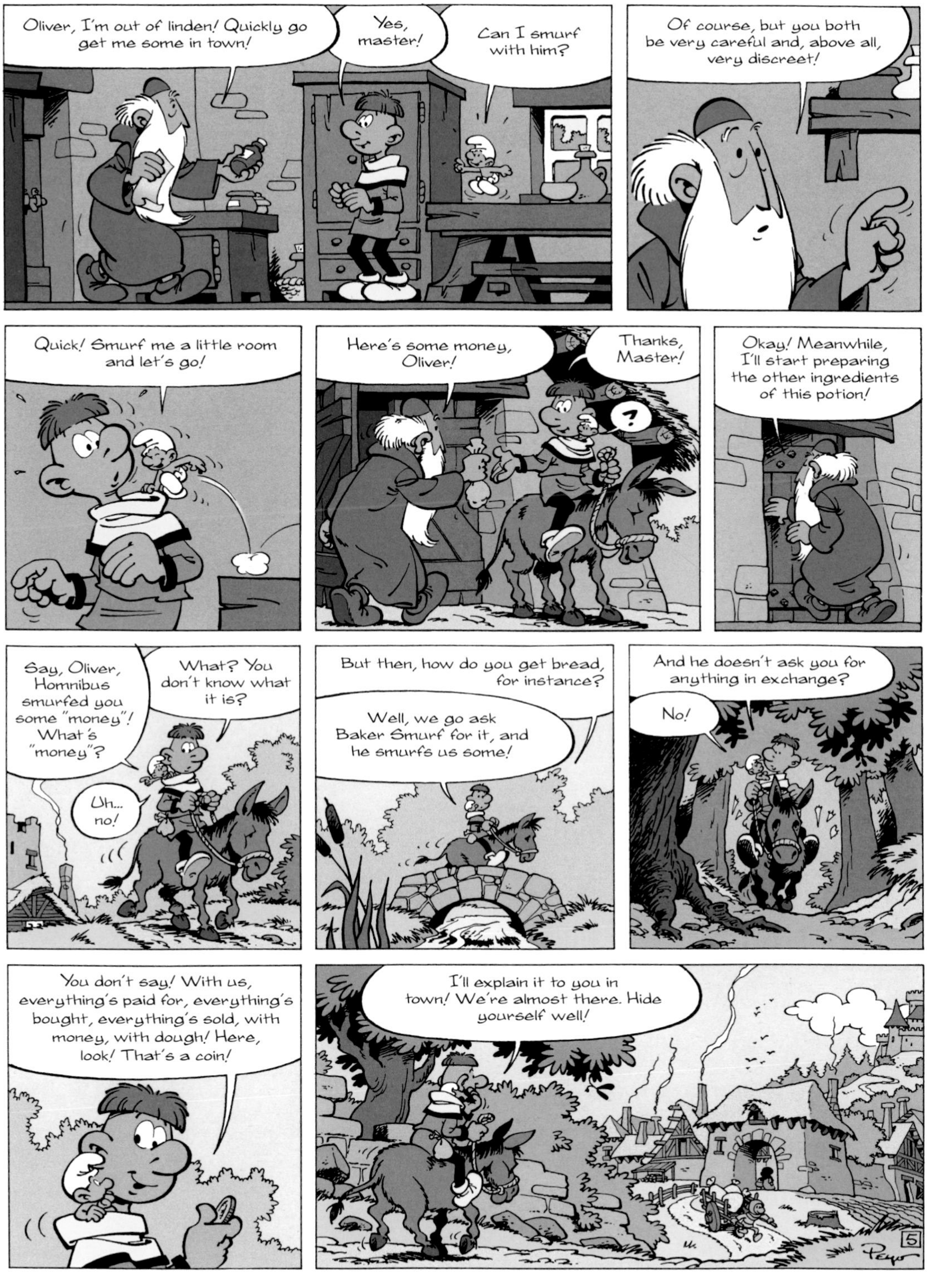
Oliver, I'm out of linden! Quickly go get me some in town!
Yes, master!
Can I smurf with him?
Of course, but you both be very careful and, above all, very discreet!
Quick! Smurf me a little room and let's go!
Here's some money, Oliver!
Thanks, Master!
?
Okay! Meanwhile, I'll start preparing the other ingredients of this potion!
Say, Oliver, Homnibus smurfed you some "money"! What's "money"?
What? You don't know what it is?
Uh... no!
But then, how do you get bread, for instance?
Well, we go ask Baker Smurf for it, and he smurfs us some!
And he doesn't ask you for anything in exchange?
No!
You don't say! With us, everything's paid for, everything's bought, everything's sold, with money, with dough! Here, look! That's a coin!
I'll explain it to you in town! We're almost there. Hide yourself well!
5
Peyo

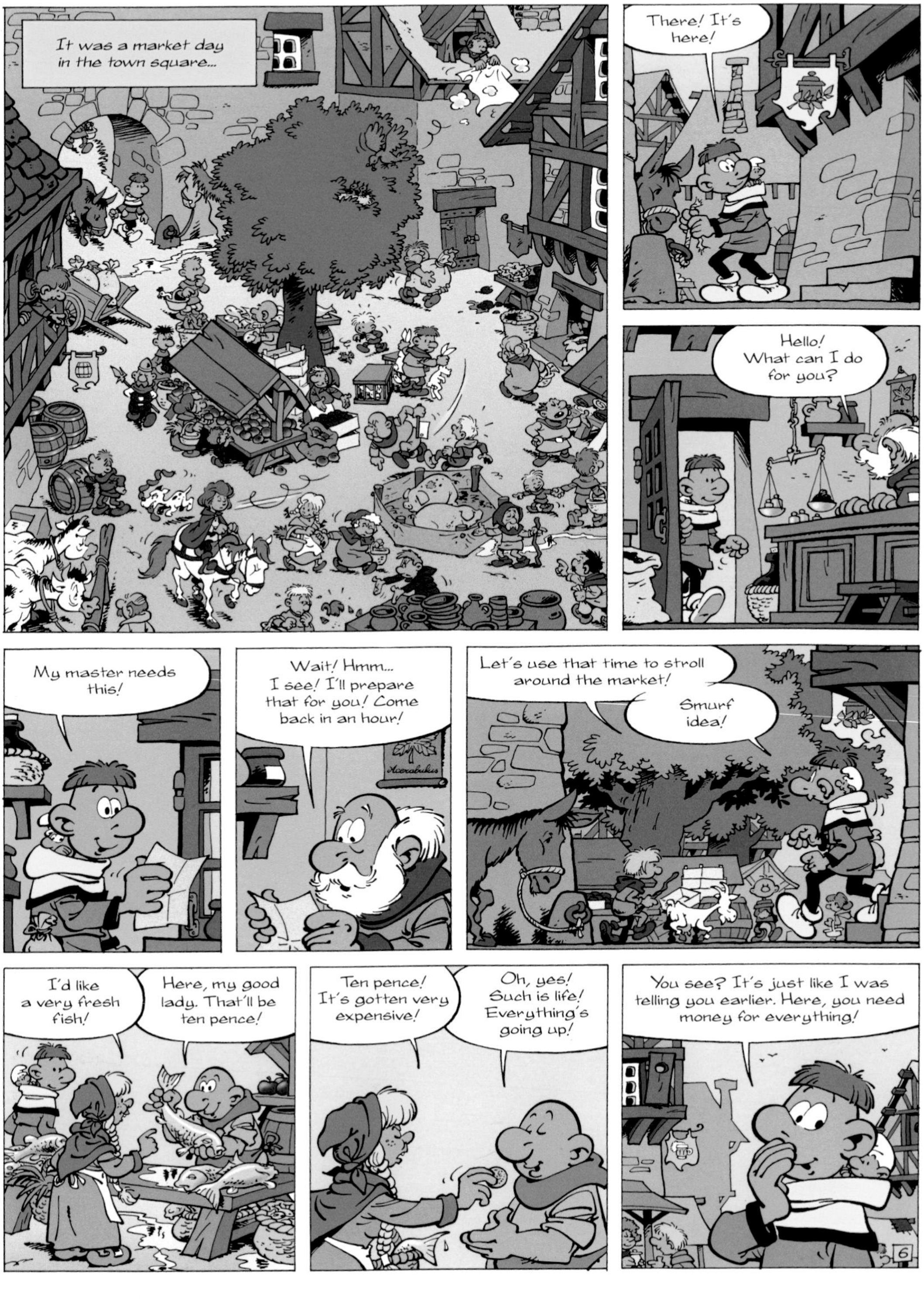

It was a market day in the town square...
There! It's here!
Hello! What can I do for you?
My master needs this!
Wait! Hmm... I see! I'll prepare that for you! Come back in an hour!
Acerabukus
Let's use that time to stroll around the market!
Smurf idea!
I'd like a very fresh fish!
Here, my good lady. That'll be ten pence!
Ten pence! It's gotten very expensive!
Oh, yes! Such is life! Everything's going up!
You see? It's just like I was telling you earlier. Here, you need money for everything!
6

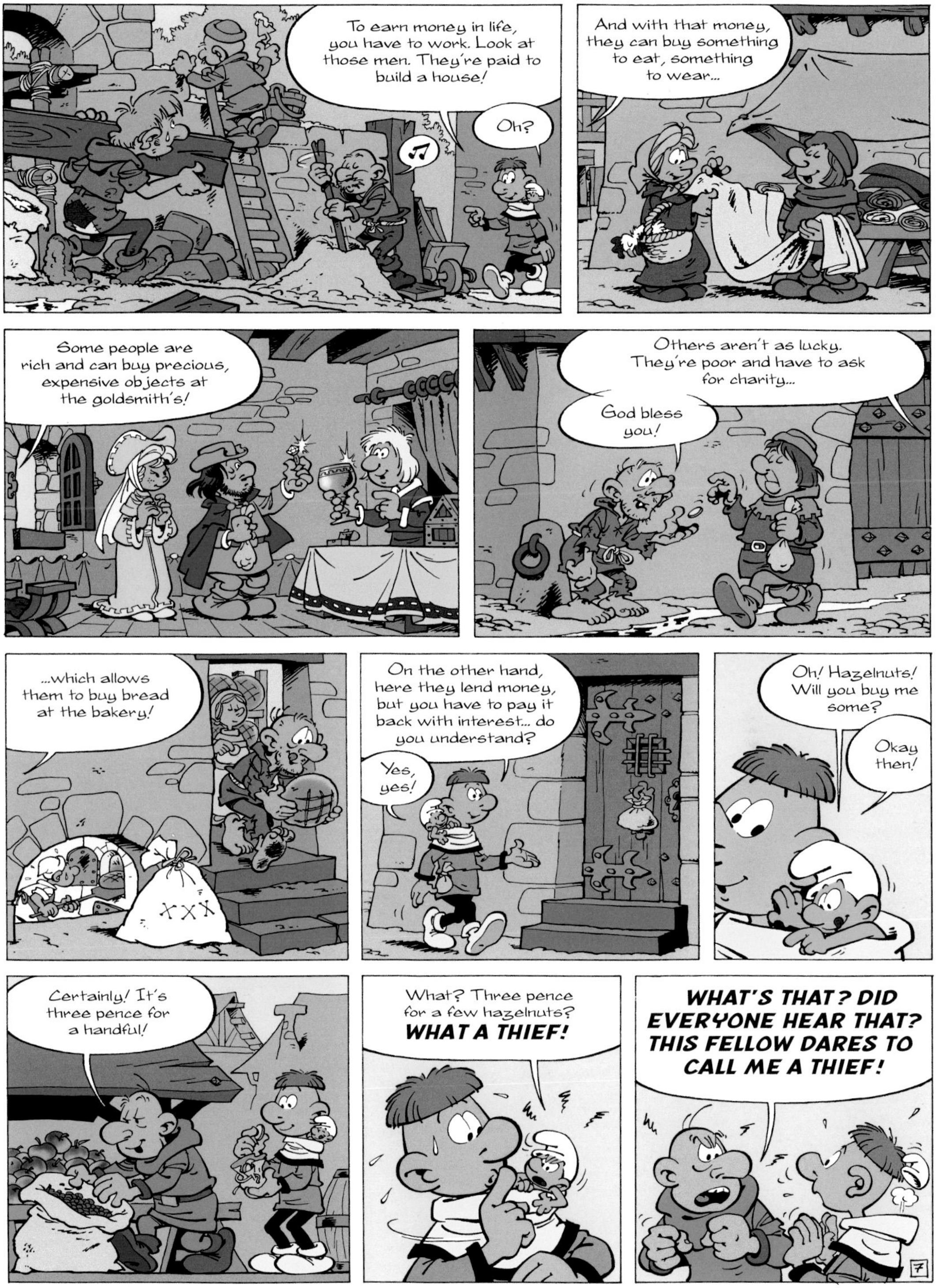

To earn money in life, you have to work. Look at those men. They're paid to build a house!
Oh?
And with that money, they can buy something to eat, something to wear...
Some people are rich and can buy precious, expensive objects at the goldsmith's!
Others aren't as lucky. They're poor and have to ask for charity...
God bless you!
...which allows them to buy bread at the bakery!
On the other hand, here they lend money, but you have to pay it back with interest... do you understand?
Yes, yes!
Oh! Hazelnuts! Will you buy me some?
Okay then!
Certainly! It's three pence for a handful!
What? Three pence for a few hazelnuts? **WHAT A THIEF!**
WHAT'S THAT? DID EVERYONE HEAR THAT? THIS FELLOW DARES TO CALL ME A THIEF!
7

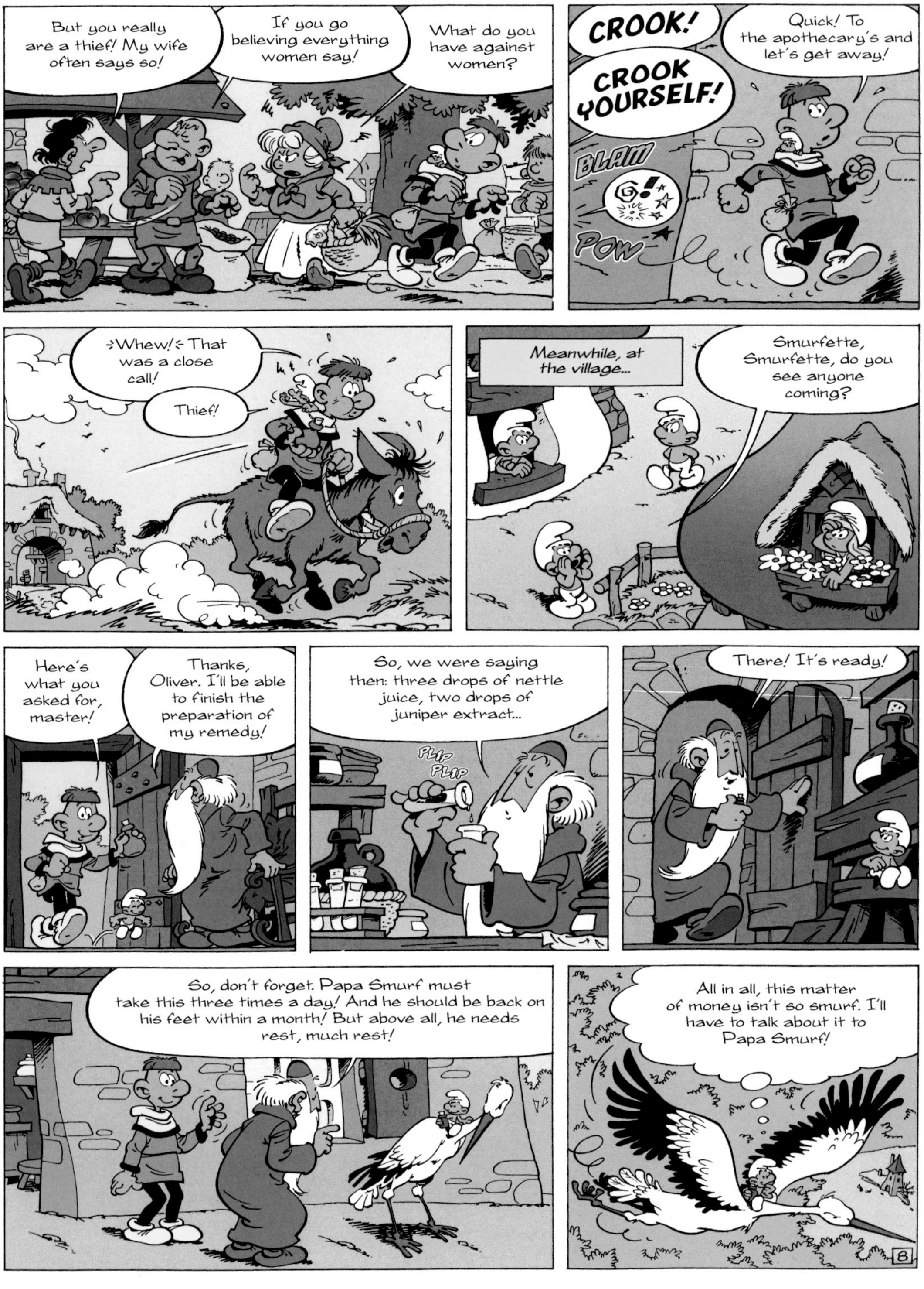

But you really are a thief! My wife often says so!
If you go believing everything women say!
What do you have against women?
CROOK!
CROOK YOURSELF!
BLAM
POW
Quick! To the apothecary's and let's get away!
Whew! That was a close call!
Thief!
Meanwhile, at the village...
Smurfette, Smurfette, do you see anyone coming?
Here's what you asked for, master!
Thanks, Oliver. I'll be able to finish the preparation of my remedy!
So, we were saying then: three drops of nettle juice, two drops of juniper extract...
PLIP PLIP
There! It's ready!
So, don't forget. Papa Smurf must take this three times a day! And he should be back on his feet within a month! But above all, he needs rest, much rest!
All in all, this matter of money isn't so smurf. I'll have to talk about it to Papa Smurf!
8

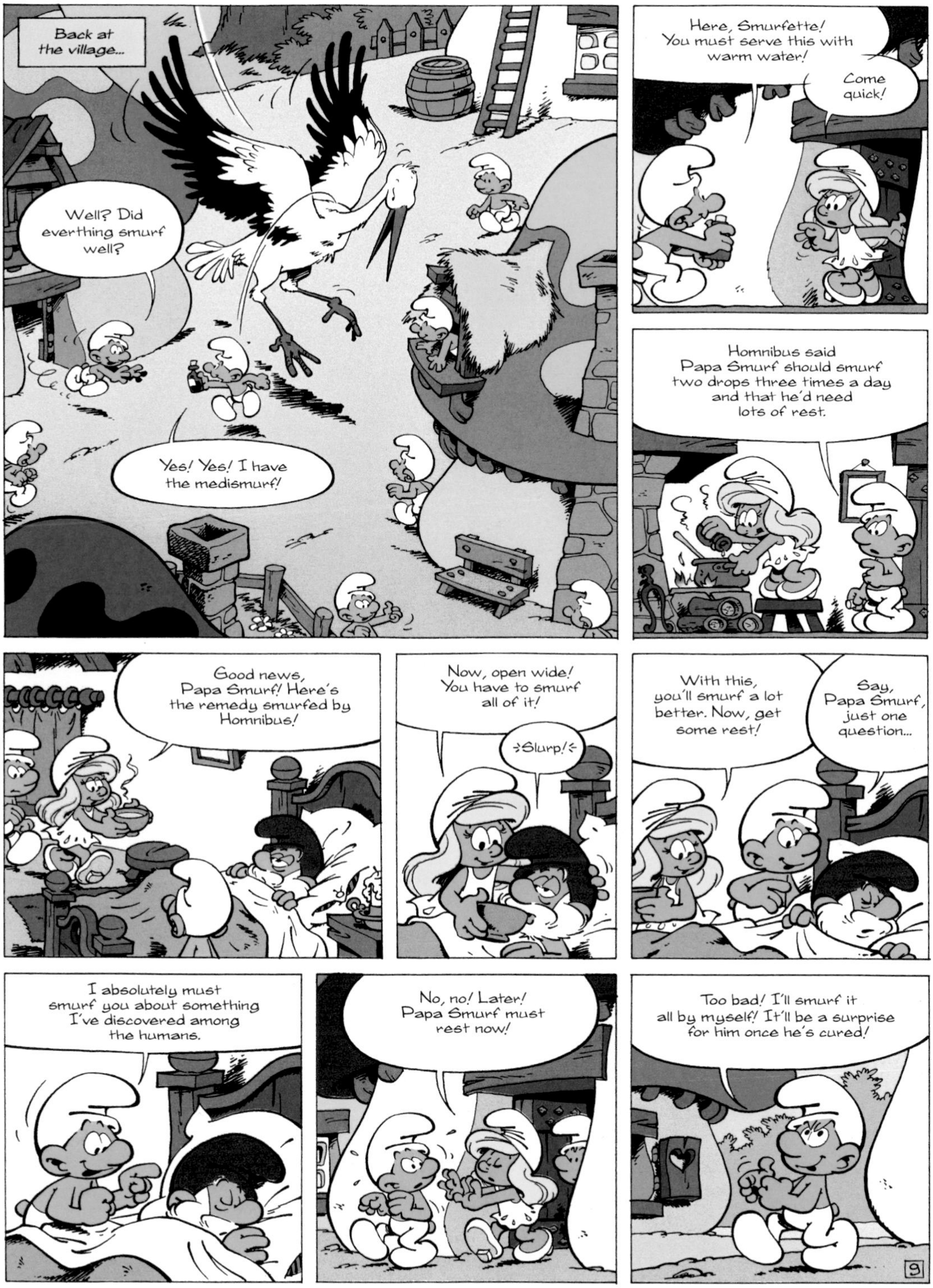
Back at the village...
Well? Did everthing smurf well?
Yes! Yes! I have the medismurf!
Here, Smurfette! You must serve this with warm water!
Come quick!
Homnibus said Papa Smurf should smurf two drops three times a day and that he'd need lots of rest.
Good news, Papa Smurf! Here's the remedy smurfed by Homnibus!
Now, open wide! You have to smurf all of it!
Slurp!
With this, you'll smurf a lot better. Now, get some rest!
Say, Papa Smurf, just one question...
I absolutely must smurf you about something I've discovered among the humans.
No, no! Later! Papa Smurf must rest now!
Too bad! I'll smurf it all by myself! It'll be a surprise for him once he's cured!
9

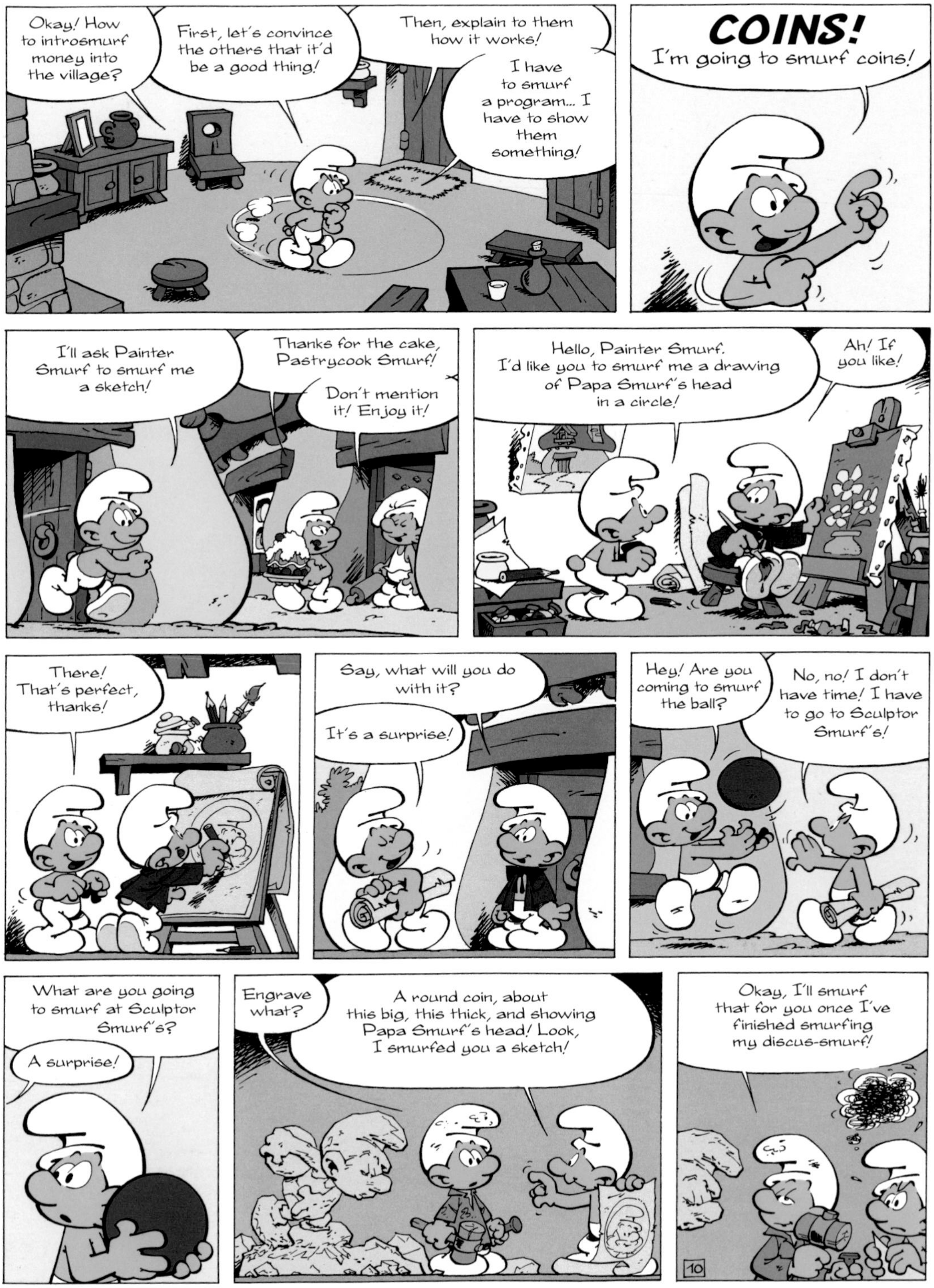
Okay! How to introsmurf money into the village?
First, let's convince the others that it'd be a good thing!
Then, explain to them how it works!
I have to smurf a program... I have to show them something!
COINS!
I'm going to smurf coins!
I'll ask Painter Smurf to smurf me a sketch!
Thanks for the cake, Pastrycook Smurf!
Don't mention it! Enjoy it!
Hello, Painter Smurf. I'd like you to smurf me a drawing of Papa Smurf's head in a circle!
Ah! If you like!
There! That's perfect, thanks!
Say, what will you do with it?
It's a surprise!
Hey! Are you coming to smurf the ball?
No, no! I don't have time! I have to go to Sculptor Smurf's!
What are you going to smurf at Sculptor Smurf's?
A surprise!
Engrave what?
A round coin, about this big, this thick, and showing Papa Smurf's head! Look, I smurfed you a sketch!
Okay, I'll smurf that for you once I've finished smurfing my discus-smurf!
10

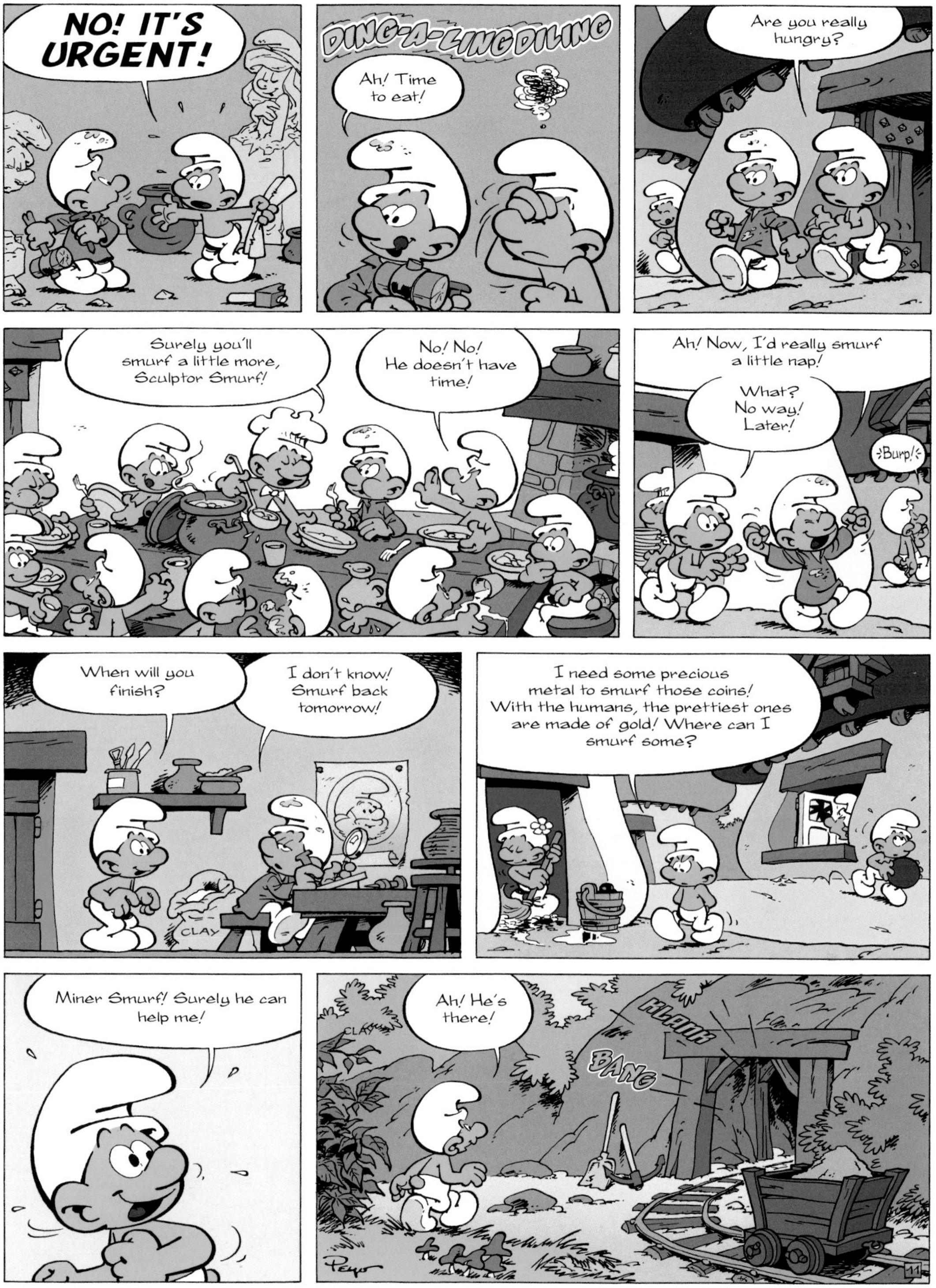

NO! IT'S URGENT!
DING-A-LING DILING
Ah! Time to eat!
Are you really hungry?
Surely you'll smurf a little more, Sculptor Smurf!
No! No! He doesn't have time!
Ah! Now, I'd really smurf a little nap!
What? No way! Later!
Burp!
When will you finish?
I don't know! Smurf back tomorrow!
CLAY
I need some precious metal to smurf those coins! With the humans, the prettiest ones are made of gold! Where can I smurf some?
Miner Smurf! Surely he can help me!
Ah! He's there!
KLANK
BANG
Peyo
11

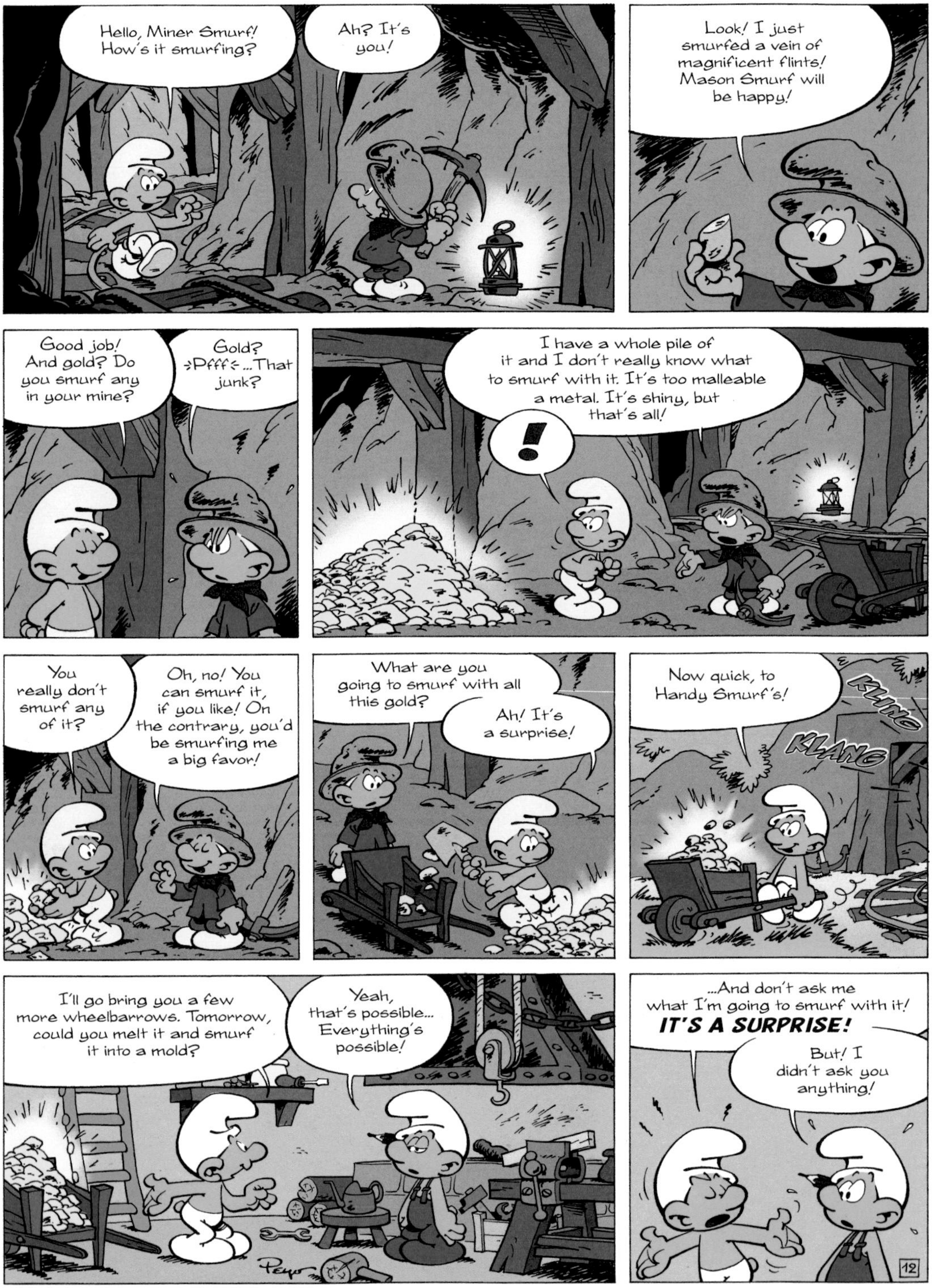
Hello, Miner Smurf! How's it smurfing?
Ah? It's you!
Look! I just smurfed a vein of magnificent flints! Mason Smurf will be happy!
Good job! And gold? Do you smurf any in your mine?
Gold? ⪢Pfff⪡ ...That junk?
I have a whole pile of it and I don't really know what to smurf with it. It's too malleable a metal. It's shiny, but that's all!
!
You really don't smurf any of it?
Oh, no! You can smurf it, if you like! On the contrary, you'd be smurfing me a big favor!
What are you going to smurf with all this gold?
Ah! It's a surprise!
Now quick, to Handy Smurf's!
KLING
KLANG
I'll go bring you a few more wheelbarrows. Tomorrow, could you melt it and smurf it into a mold?
Yeah, that's possible... Everything's possible!
Peyo
...And don't ask me what I'm going to smurf with it!
IT'S A SURPRISE!
But! I didn't ask you anything!
12

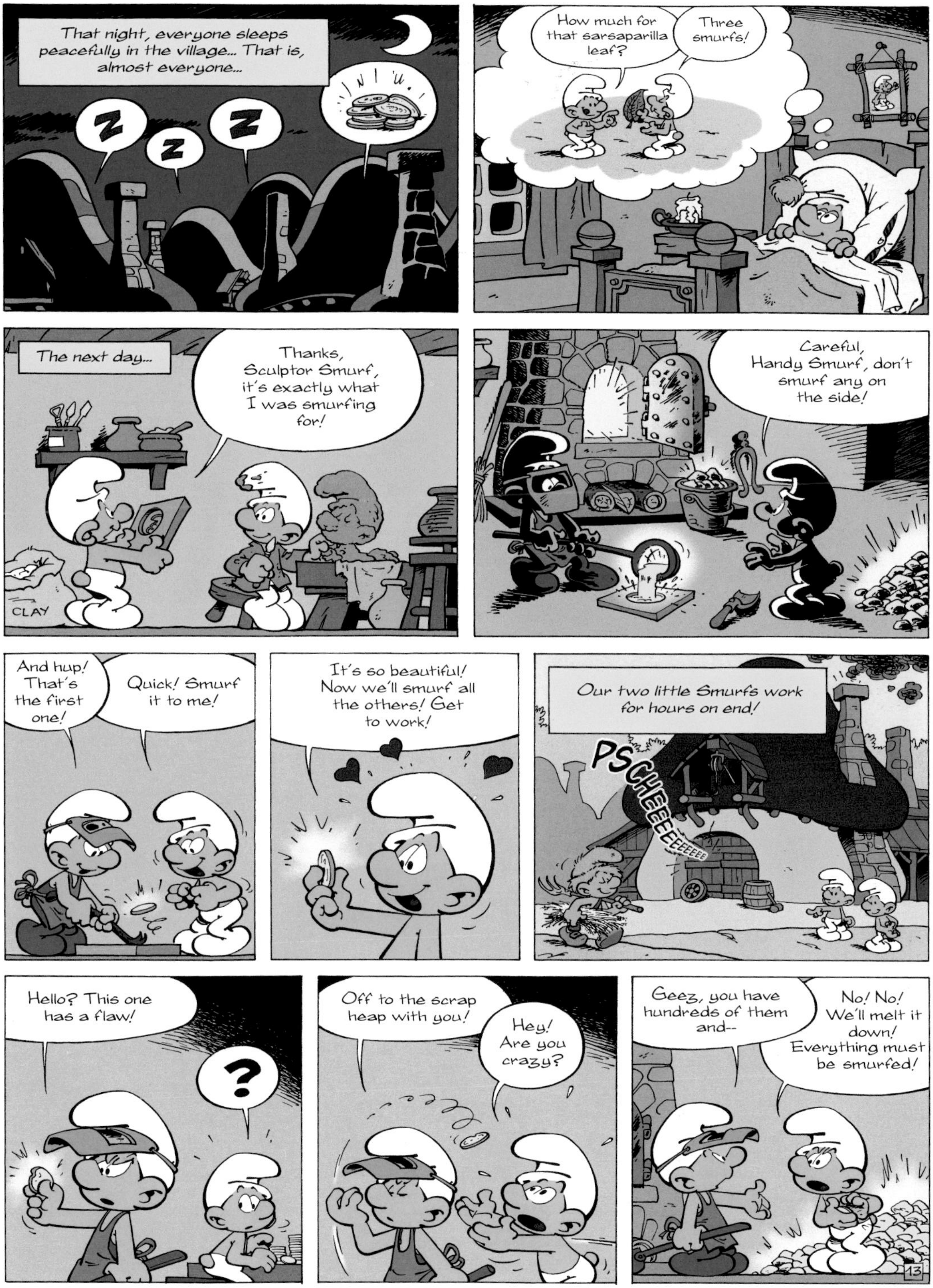
That night, everyone sleeps peacefully in the village... That is, almost everyone...
Z
Z
Z
How much for that sarsaparilla leaf?
Three smurfs!
The next day...
Thanks, Sculptor Smurf, it's exactly what I was smurfing for!
CLAY
Careful, Handy Smurf, don't smurf any on the side!
And hup! That's the first one!
Quick! Smurf it to me!
It's so beautiful! Now we'll smurf all the others! Get to work!
Our two little Smurfs work for hours on end!
PSCHEEEEEEEEEE
Hello? This one has a flaw!
?
Off to the scrap heap with you!
Hey! Are you crazy?
Geez, you have hundreds of them and--
No! No! We'll melt it down! Everything must be smurfed!
13

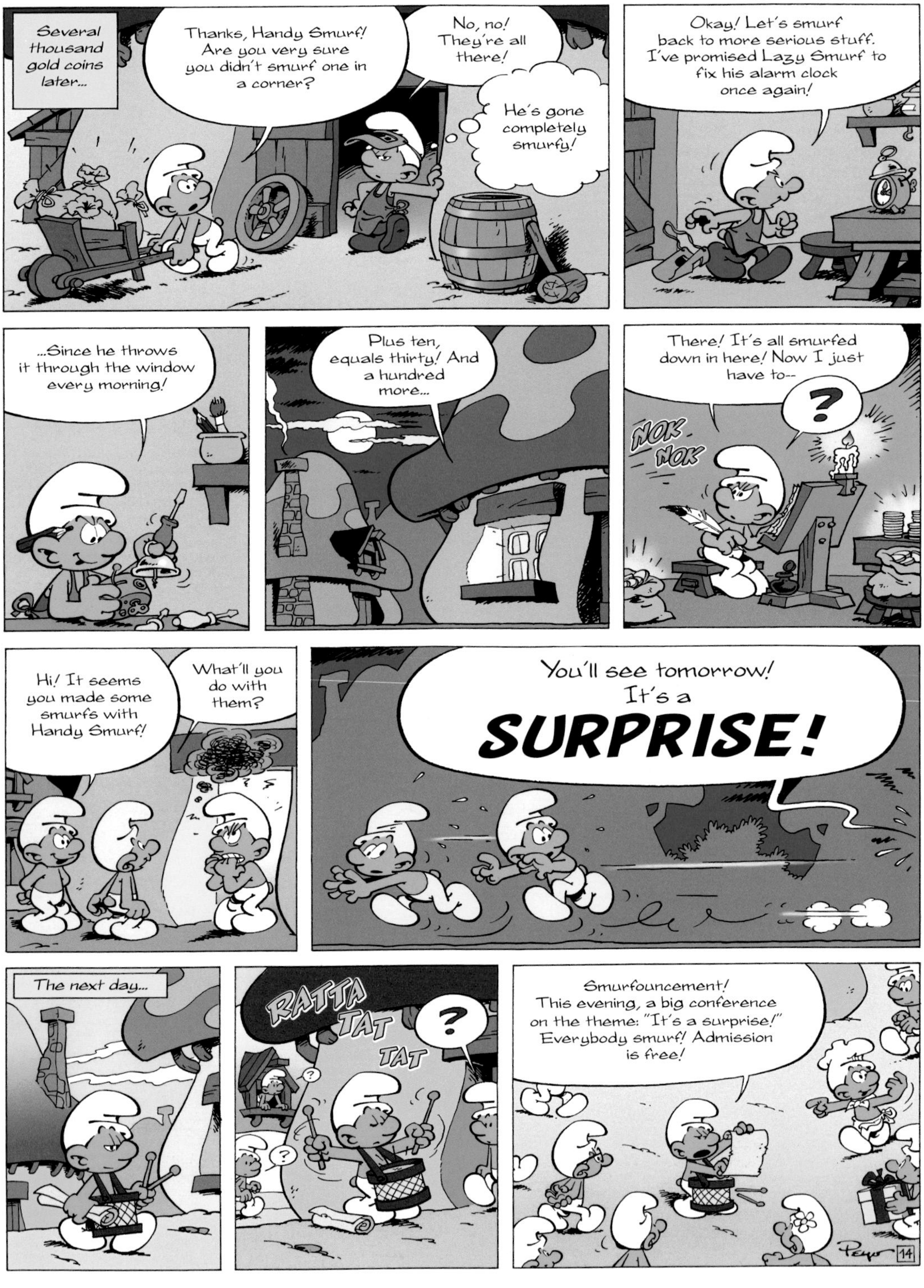

Several thousand gold coins later...
Thanks, Handy Smurf! Are you very sure you didn't smurf one in a corner?
No, no! They're all there!
He's gone completely smurfy!
Okay! Let's smurf back to more serious stuff. I've promised Lazy Smurf to fix his alarm clock once again!
...Since he throws it through the window every morning!
Plus ten, equals thirty! And a hundred more...
There! It's all smurfed down in here! Now I just have to--
NOK NOK
?
Hi! It seems you made some smurfs with Handy Smurf!
What'll you do with them?
You'll see tomorrow! It's a SURPRISE!
The next day...
RATTA TAT TAT
?
Smurfouncement! This evening, a big conference on the theme: "It's a surprise!" Everybody smurf! Admission is free!
Peyo
14

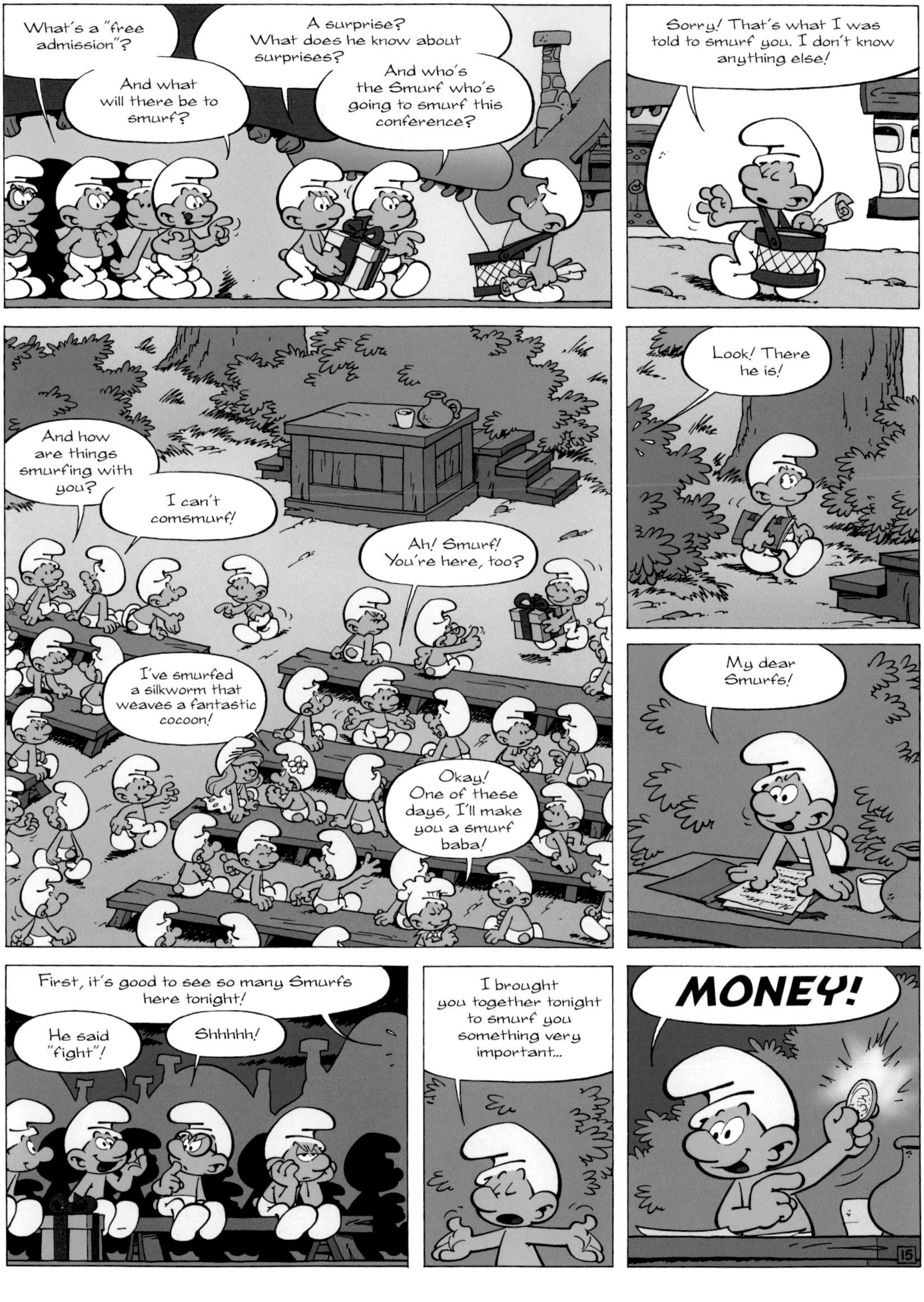

What's a "free admission"?
And what will there be to smurf?
A surprise? What does he know about surprises?
And who's the Smurf who's going to smurf this conference?
Sorry! That's what I was told to smurf you. I don't know anything else!
And how are things smurfing with you?
I can't comsmurf!
Ah! Smurf! You're here, too?
I've smurfed a silkworm that weaves a fantastic cocoon!
Okay! One of these days, I'll make you a smurf baba!
Look! There he is!
My dear Smurfs!
First, it's good to see so many Smurfs here tonight!
He said "fight"!
Shhhhh!
I brought you together tonight to smurf you something very important...
MONEY!
15

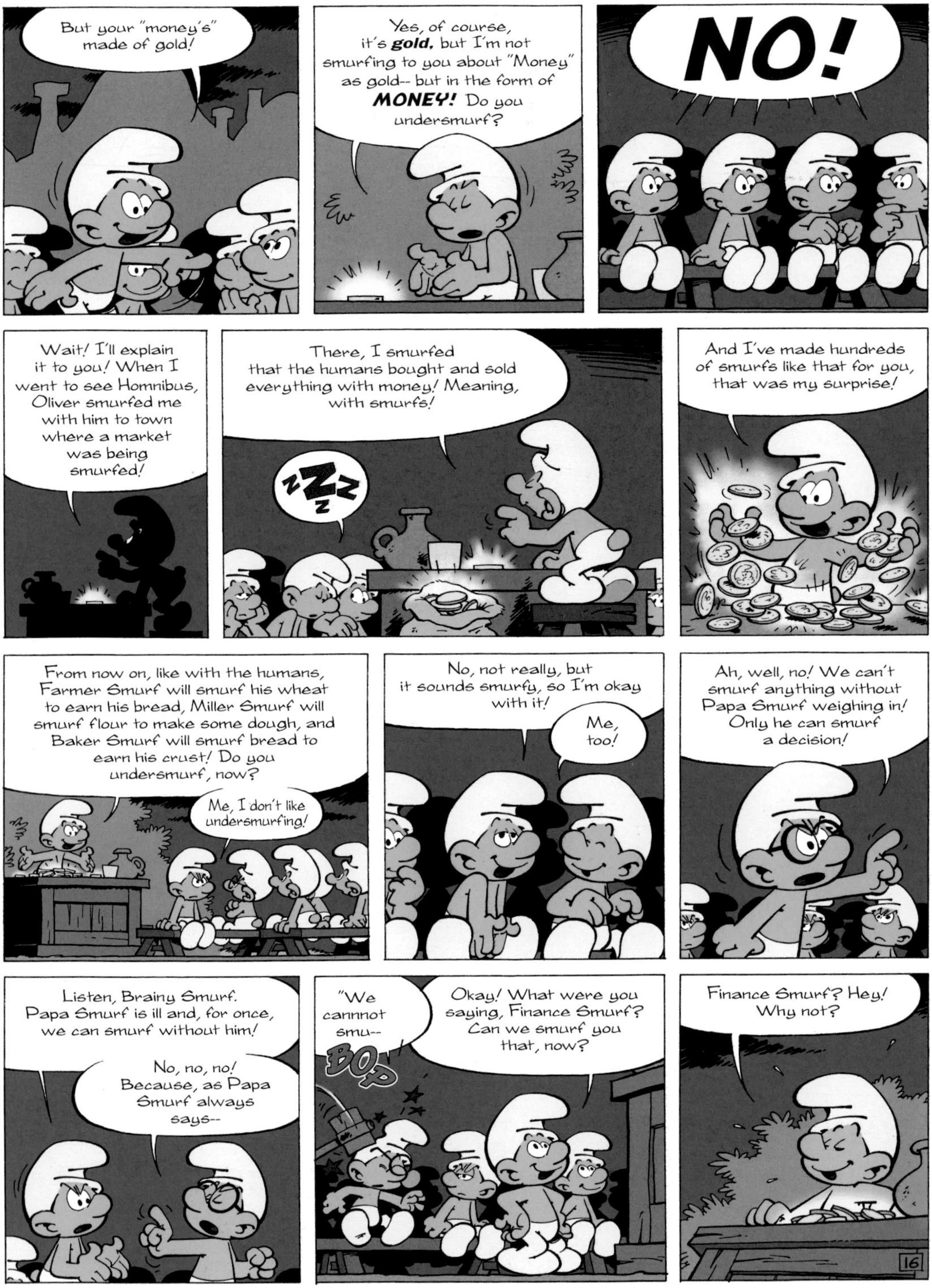
But your "money's" made of gold!
Yes, of course, it's **gold**, but I'm not smurfing to you about "Money" as gold-- but in the form of **MONEY!** Do you undersmurf?
NO!
Wait! I'll explain it to you! When I went to see Homnibus, Oliver smurfed me with him to town where a market was being smurfed!
There, I smurfed that the humans bought and sold everything with money! Meaning, with smurfs!
ZZZ
And I've made hundreds of smurfs like that for you, that was my surprise!
From now on, like with the humans, Farmer Smurf will smurf his wheat to earn his bread, Miller Smurf will smurf flour to make some dough, and Baker Smurf will smurf bread to earn his crust! Do you undersmurf, now?
Me, I don't like undersmurfing!
No, not really, but it sounds smurfy, so I'm okay with it!
Me, too!
Ah, well, no! We can't smurf anything without Papa Smurf weighing in! Only he can smurf a decision!
Listen, Brainy Smurf. Papa Smurf is ill and, for once, we can smurf without him!
No, no, no! Because, as Papa Smurf always says--
"We cannot smu--
BOP
Okay! What were you saying, Finance Smurf? Can we smurf you that, now?
Finance Smurf? Hey! Why not?
16

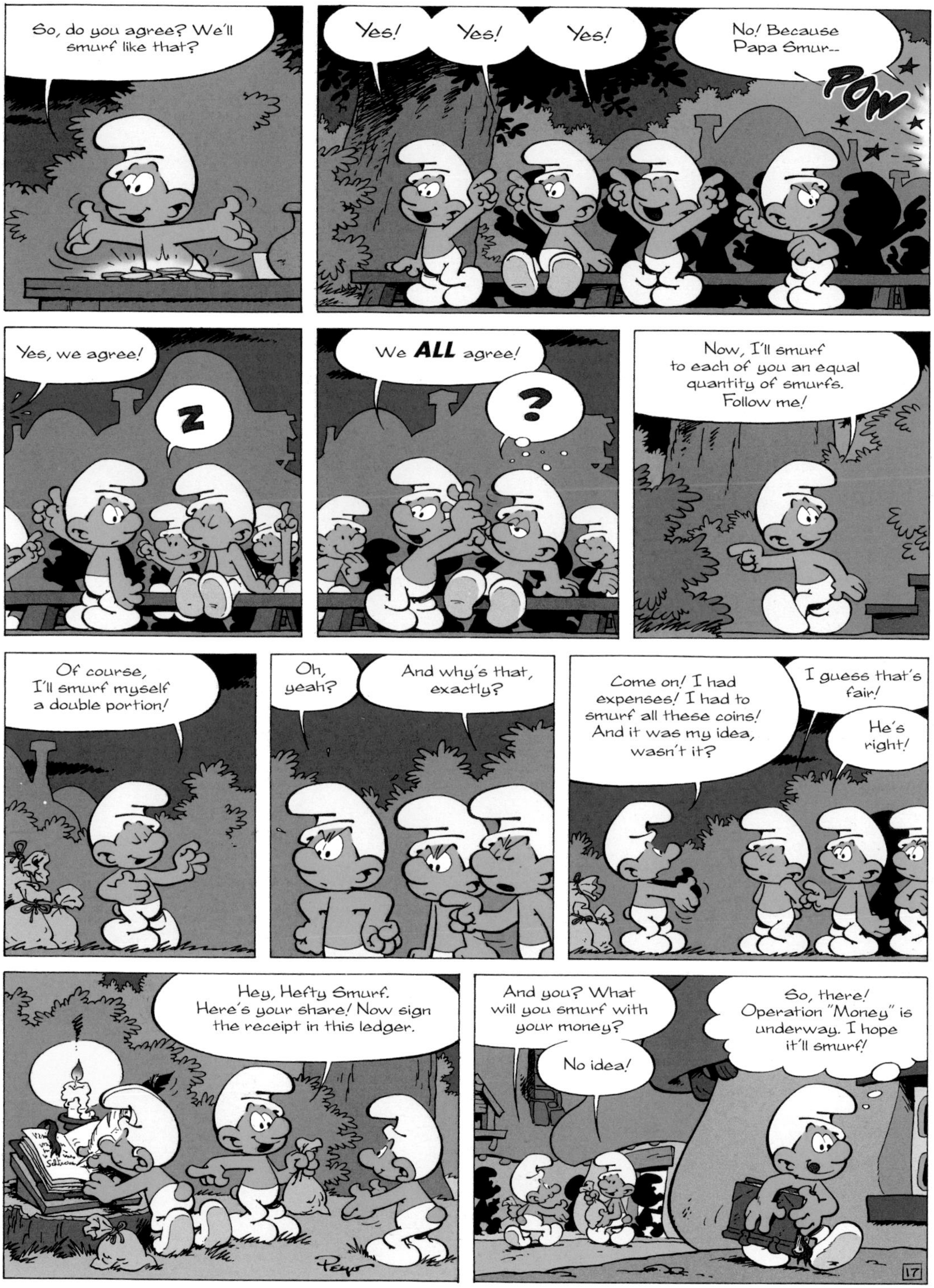
So, do you agree? We'll smurf like that?
Yes!
Yes!
Yes!
No! Because Papa Smur--
POW
Yes, we agree!
Z
We ALL agree!
?
Now, I'll smurf to each of you an equal quantity of smurfs. Follow me!
Of course, I'll smurf myself a double portion!
Oh, yeah?
And why's that, exactly?
Come on! I had expenses! I had to smurf all these coins! And it was my idea, wasn't it?
I guess that's fair!
He's right!
Hey, Hefty Smurf. Here's your share! Now sign the receipt in this ledger.
Peyo
And you? What will you smurf with your money?
No idea!
So, there! Operation "Money" is underway. I hope it'll smurf!
17

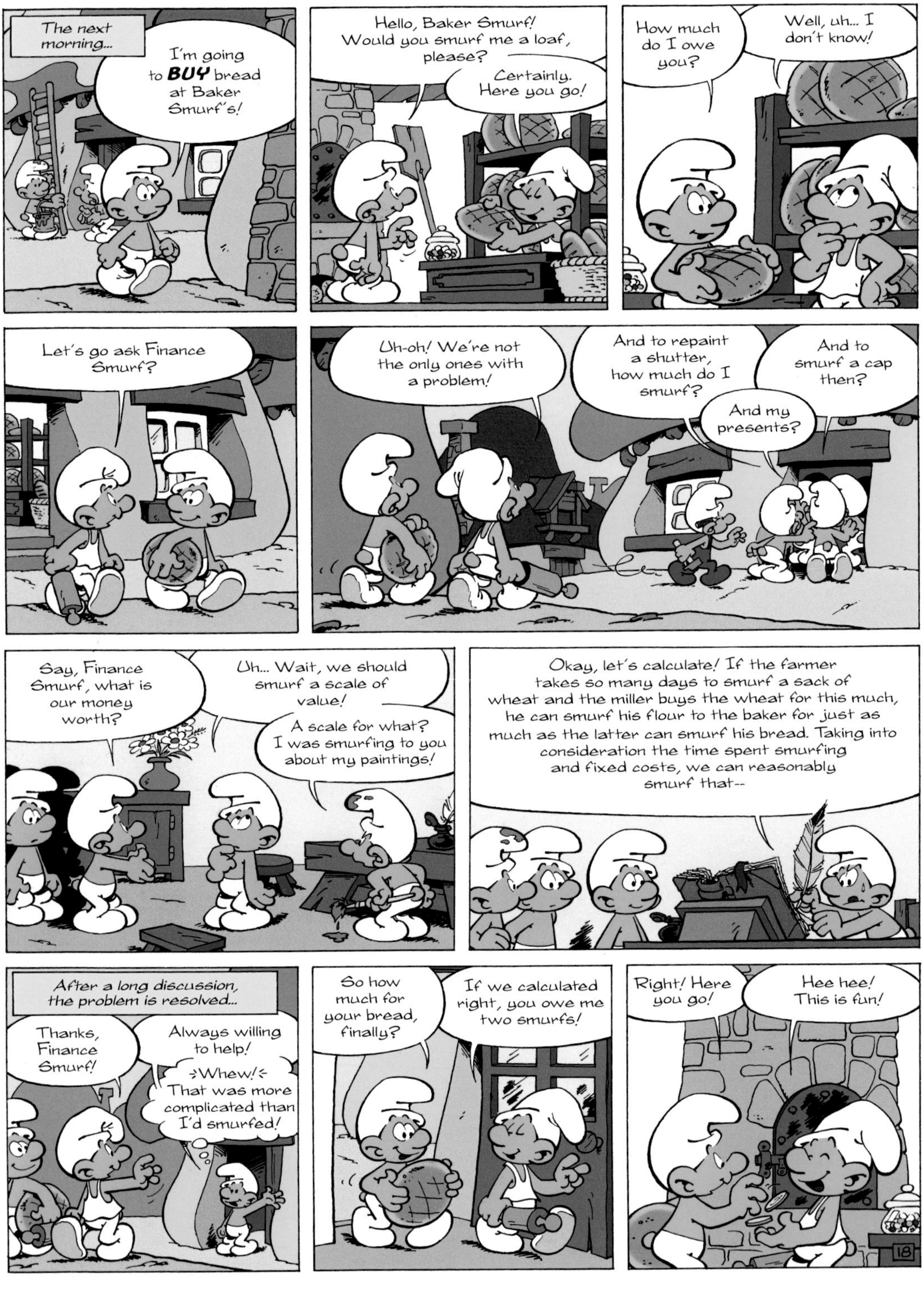
The next morning...
I'm going to **BUY** bread at Baker Smurf's!
Hello, Baker Smurf! Would you smurf me a loaf, please?
Certainly. Here you go!
How much do I owe you?
Well, uh... I don't know!
Let's go ask Finance Smurf?
Uh-oh! We're not the only ones with a problem!
And to repaint a shutter, how much do I smurf?
And to smurf a cap then?
And my presents?
Say, Finance Smurf, what is our money worth?
Uh... Wait, we should smurf a scale of value!
A scale for what? I was smurfing to you about my paintings!
Okay, let's calculate! If the farmer takes so many days to smurf a sack of wheat and the miller buys the wheat for this much, he can smurf his flour to the baker for just as much as the latter can smurf his bread. Taking into consideration the time spent smurfing and fixed costs, we can reasonably smurf that--
After a long discussion, the problem is resolved...
Thanks, Finance Smurf!
Always willing to help!
Whew! That was more complicated than I'd smurfed!
So how much for your bread, finally?
If we calculated right, you owe me two smurfs!
Right! Here you go!
Hee hee! This is fun!
18

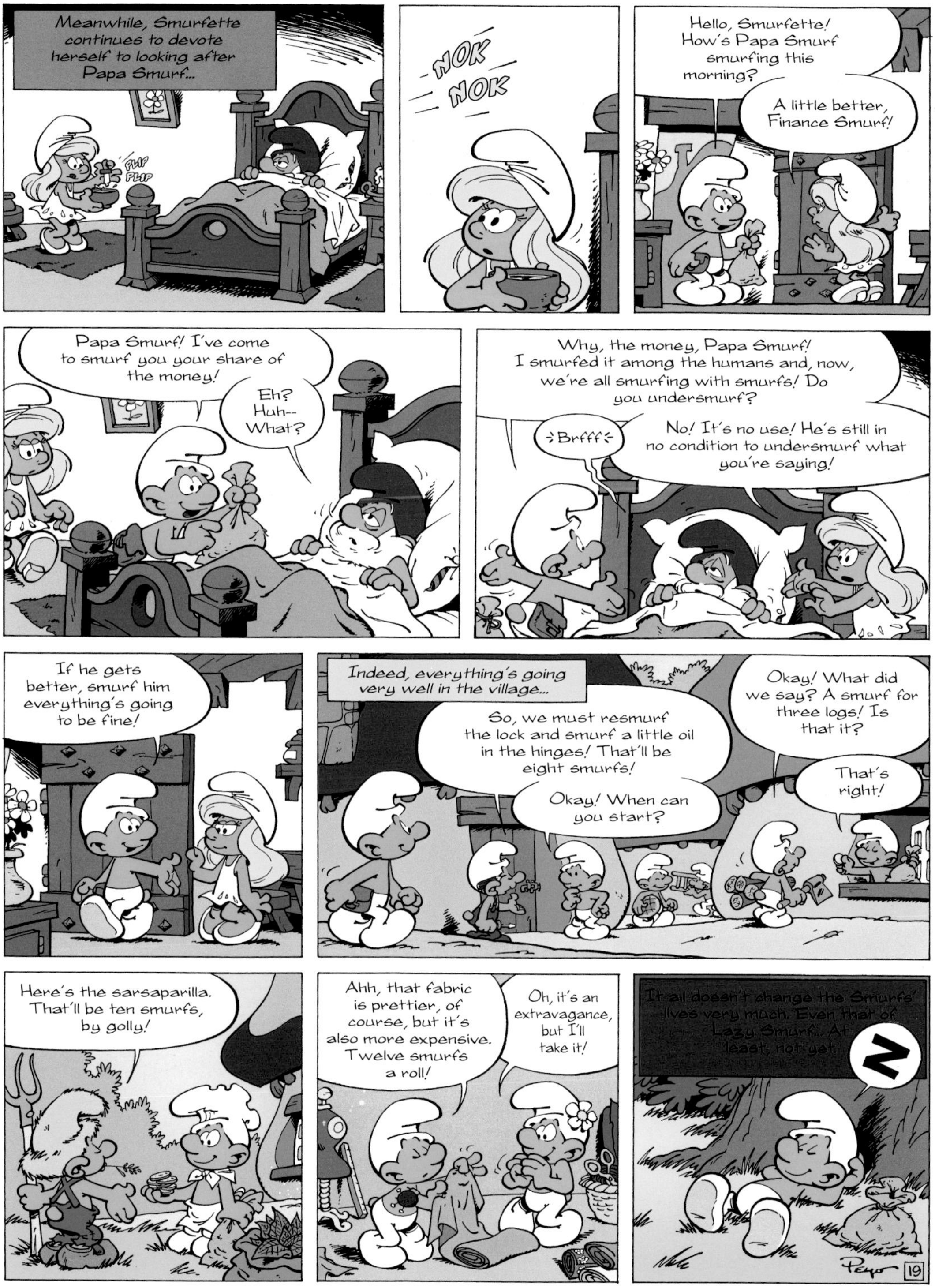

Meanwhile, Smurfette continues to devote herself to looking after Papa Smurf...
NOK NOK
Hello, Smurfette! How's Papa Smurf smurfing this morning?
A little better, Finance Smurf!
Papa Smurf! I've come to smurf you your share of the money!
Eh? Huh-- What?
Why, the money, Papa Smurf! I smurfed it among the humans and, now, we're all smurfing with smurfs! Do you undersmurf?
Brfff
No! It's no use! He's still in no condition to undersmurf what you're saying!
If he gets better, smurf him everything's going to be fine!
Indeed, everything's going very well in the village...
So, we must resmurf the lock and smurf a little oil in the hinges! That'll be eight smurfs!
Okay! When can you start?
Okay! What did we say? A smurf for three logs! Is that it?
That's right!
Here's the sarsaparilla. That'll be ten smurfs, by golly!
Ahh, that fabric is prettier, of course, but it's also more expensive. Twelve smurfs a roll!
Oh, it's an extravagance, but I'll take it!
It all doesn't change the Smurfs' lives very much. Even that of Lazy Smurf... At least, not yet.
Z
Peyo
19

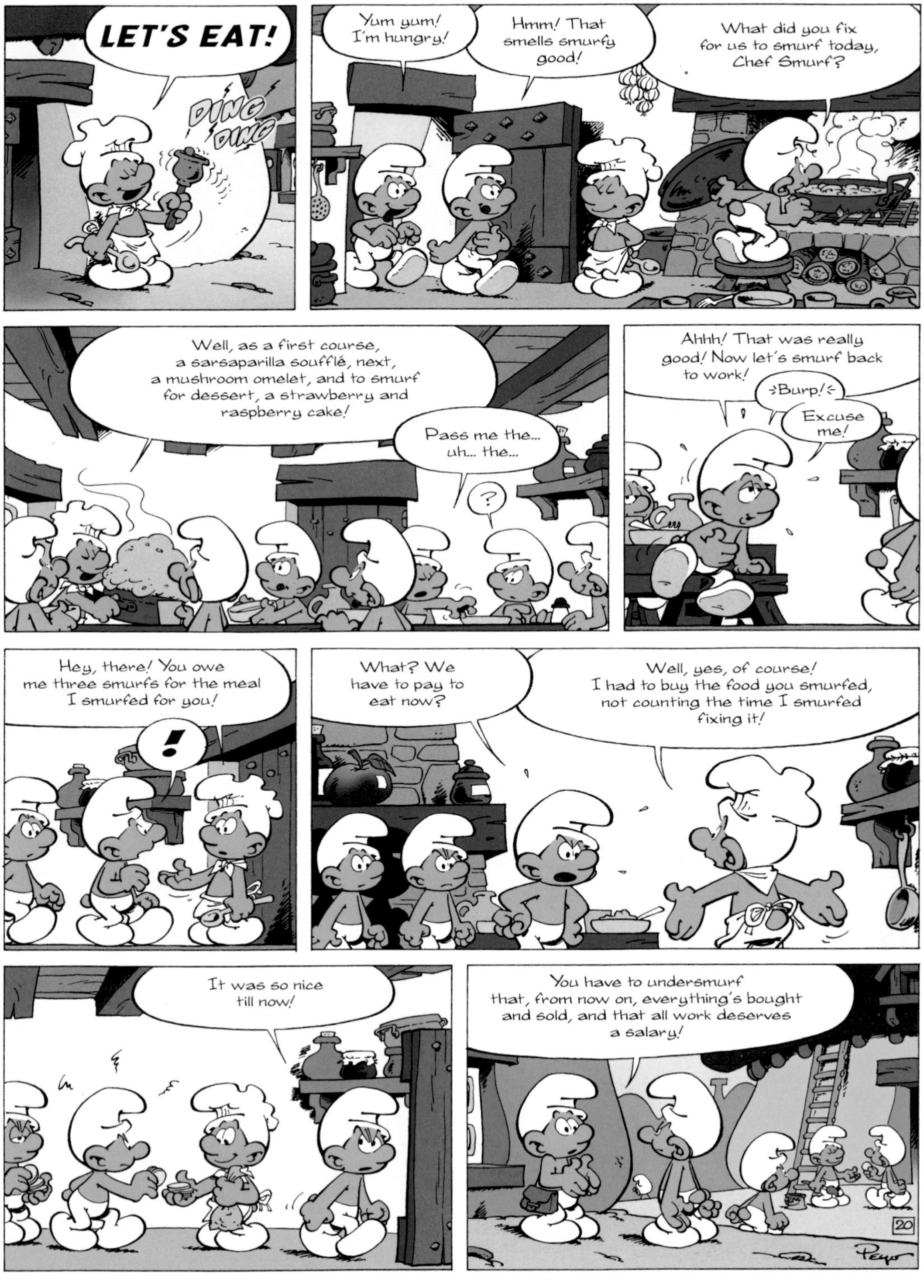
LET'S EAT!
DING DING
Yum yum! I'm hungry!
Hmm! That smells smurfy good!
What did you fix for us to smurf today, Chef Smurf?
Well, as a first course, a sarsaparilla soufflé, next, a mushroom omelet, and to smurf for dessert, a strawberry and raspberry cake!
Pass me the... uh... the...
?
Ahhh! That was really good! Now let's smurf back to work!
Burp!
Excuse me!
Hey, there! You owe me three smurfs for the meal I smurfed for you!
!
What? We have to pay to eat now?
Well, yes, of course! I had to buy the food you smurfed, not counting the time I smurfed fixing it!
It was so nice till now!
You have to undersmurf that, from now on, everything's bought and sold, and that all work deserves a salary!
20
Peyo

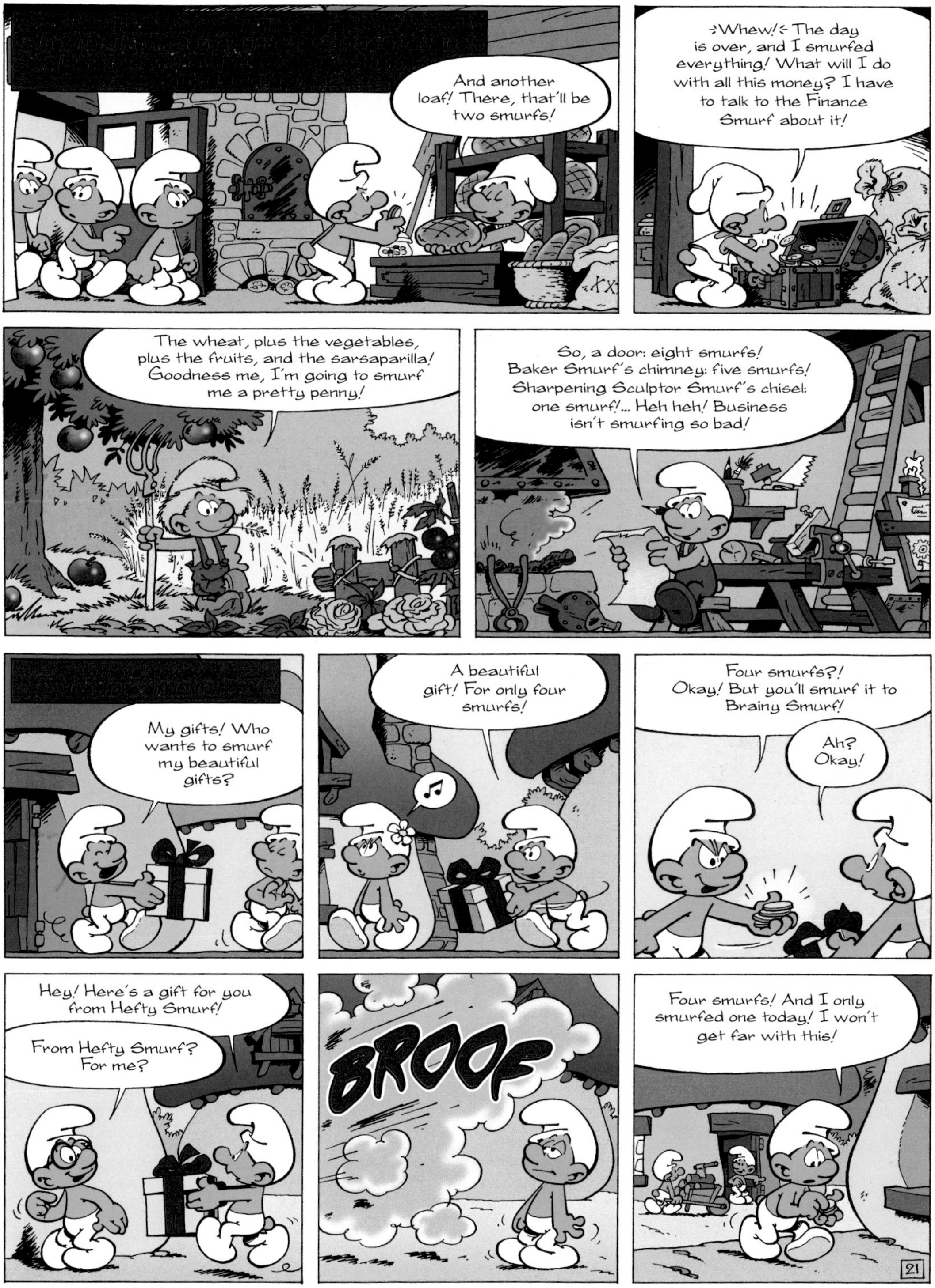
[redacted]
And another loaf! There, that'll be two smurfs!
-:Whew!:- The day is over, and I smurfed everything! What will I do with all this money? I have to talk to the Finance Smurf about it!
The wheat, plus the vegetables, plus the fruits, and the sarsaparilla! Goodness me, I'm going to smurf me a pretty penny!
So, a door: eight smurfs! Baker Smurf's chimney: five smurfs! Sharpening Sculptor Smurf's chisel: one smurf!... Heh heh! Business isn't smurfing so bad!
[redacted]
My gifts! Who wants to smurf my beautiful gifts?
A beautiful gift! For only four smurfs!
Four smurfs?! Okay! But you'll smurf it to Brainy Smurf!
Ah? Okay!
Hey! Here's a gift for you from Hefty Smurf!
From Hefty Smurf? For me?
BROOF
Four smurfs! And I only smurfed one today! I won't get far with this!
21

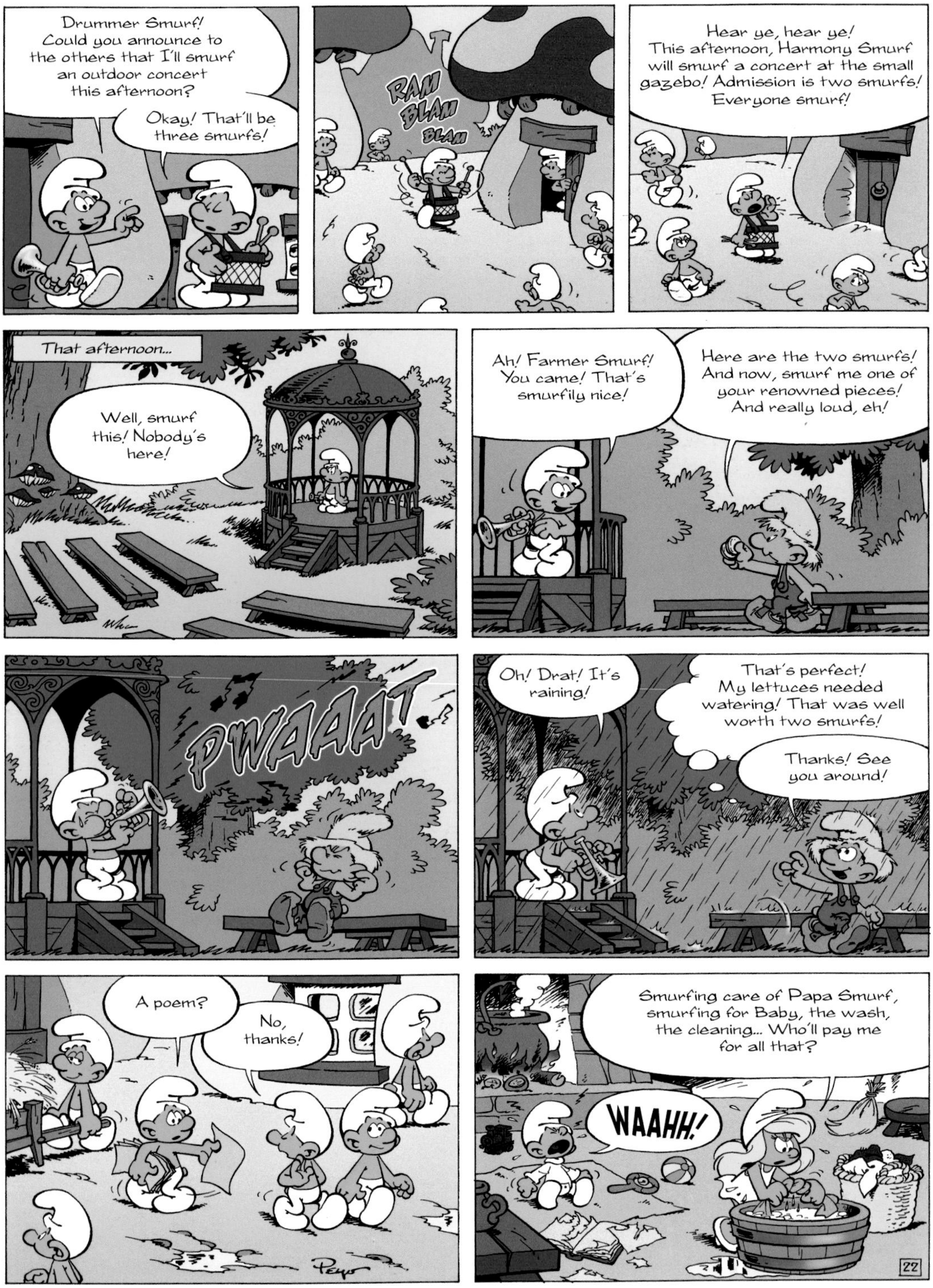
Drummer Smurf! Could you announce to the others that I'll smurf an outdoor concert this afternoon?
Okay! That'll be three smurfs!
RAM BLAM BLAM
Hear ye, hear ye! This afternoon, Harmony Smurf will smurf a concert at the small gazebo! Admission is two smurfs! Everyone smurf!
That afternoon...
Well, smurf this! Nobody's here!
Ah! Farmer Smurf! You came! That's smurfily nice!
Here are the two smurfs! And now, smurf me one of your renowned pieces! And really loud, eh!
PWAAAT
Oh! Drat! It's raining!
That's perfect! My lettuces needed watering! That was well worth two smurfs!
Thanks! See you around!
A poem?
No, thanks!
Smurfing care of Papa Smurf, smurfing for Baby, the wash, the cleaning... Who'll pay me for all that?
WAAHH!
22

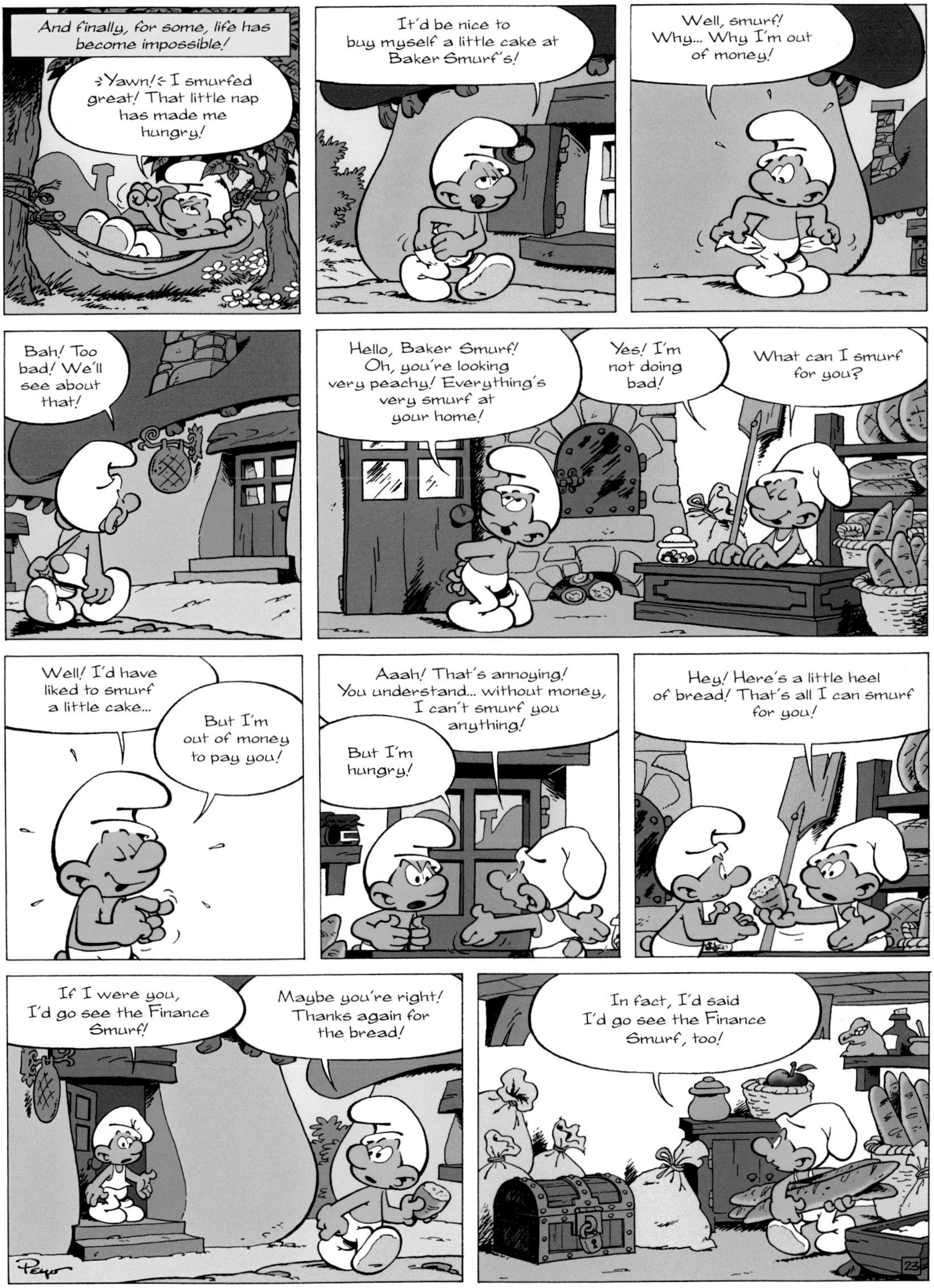
And finally, for some, life has become impossible!
⊰Yawn!⊱ I smurfed great! That little nap has made me hungry!
It'd be nice to buy myself a little cake at Baker Smurf's!
Well, smurf! Why... Why I'm out of money!
Bah! Too bad! We'll see about that!
Hello, Baker Smurf! Oh, you're looking very peachy! Everything's very smurf at your home!
Yes! I'm not doing bad!
What can I smurf for you?
Well! I'd have liked to smurf a little cake...
But I'm out of money to pay you!
Aaah! That's annoying! You understand... without money, I can't smurf you anything!
But I'm hungry!
Hey! Here's a little heel of bread! That's all I can smurf for you!
If I were you, I'd go see the Finance Smurf!
Maybe you're right! Thanks again for the bread!
In fact, I'd said I'd go see the Finance Smurf, too!

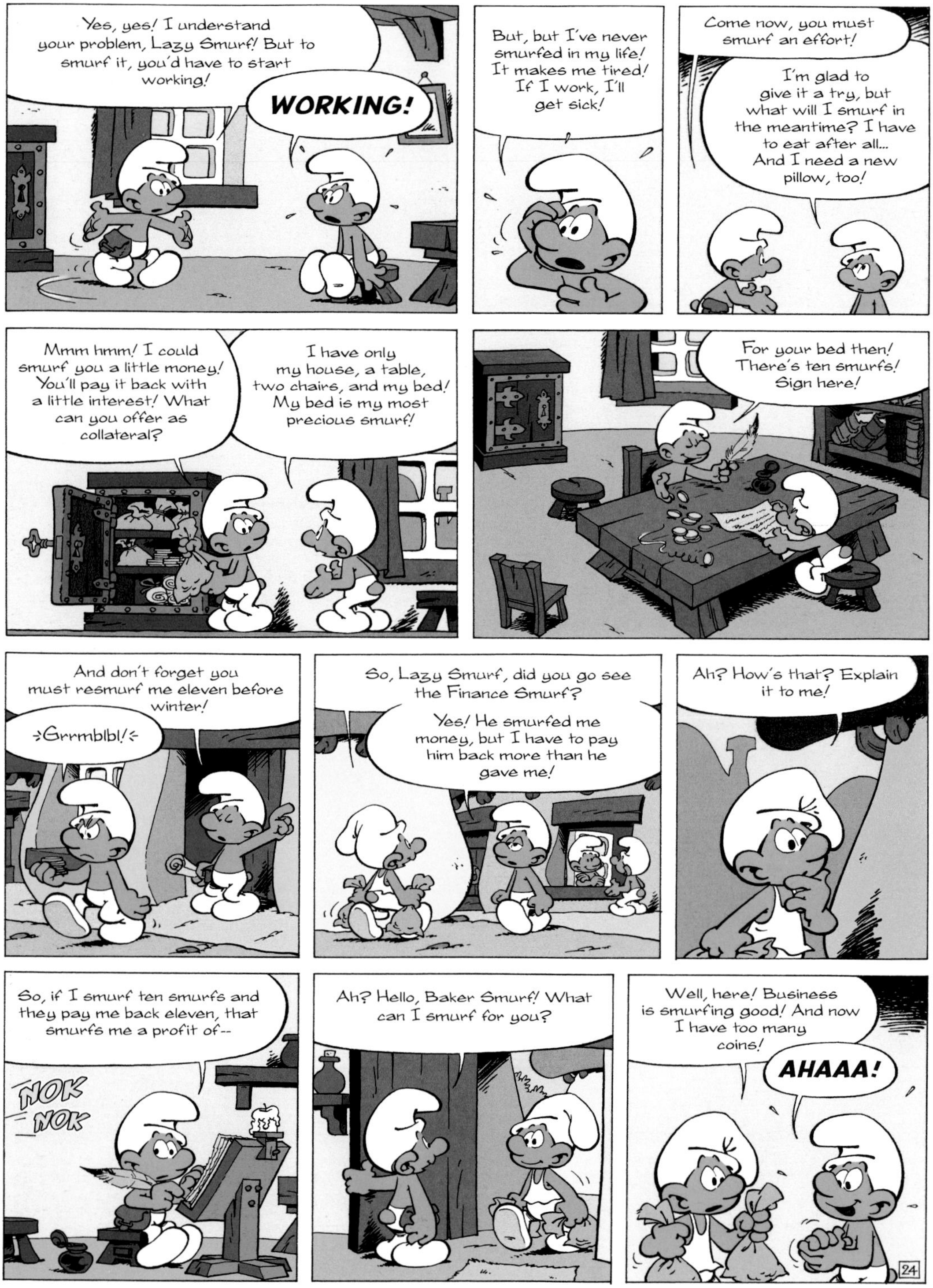

Yes, yes! I understand your problem, Lazy Smurf! But to smurf it, you'd have to start working!
WORKING!
But, but I've never smurfed in my life! It makes me tired! If I work, I'll get sick!
Come now, you must smurf an effort!
I'm glad to give it a try, but what will I smurf in the meantime? I have to eat after all... And I need a new pillow, too!
Mmm hmm! I could smurf you a little money! You'll pay it back with a little interest! What can you offer as collateral?
I have only my house, a table, two chairs, and my bed! My bed is my most precious smurf!
For your bed then! There's ten smurfs! Sign here!
And don't forget you must resmurf me eleven before winter!
Grrmblbl!
So, Lazy Smurf, did you go see the Finance Smurf?
Yes! He smurfed me money, but I have to pay him back more than he gave me!
Ah? How's that? Explain it to me!
So, if I smurf ten smurfs and they pay me back eleven, that smurfs me a profit of--
NOK NOK
Ah? Hello, Baker Smurf! What can I smurf for you?
Well, here! Business is smurfing good! And now I have too many coins!
AHAAA!
24

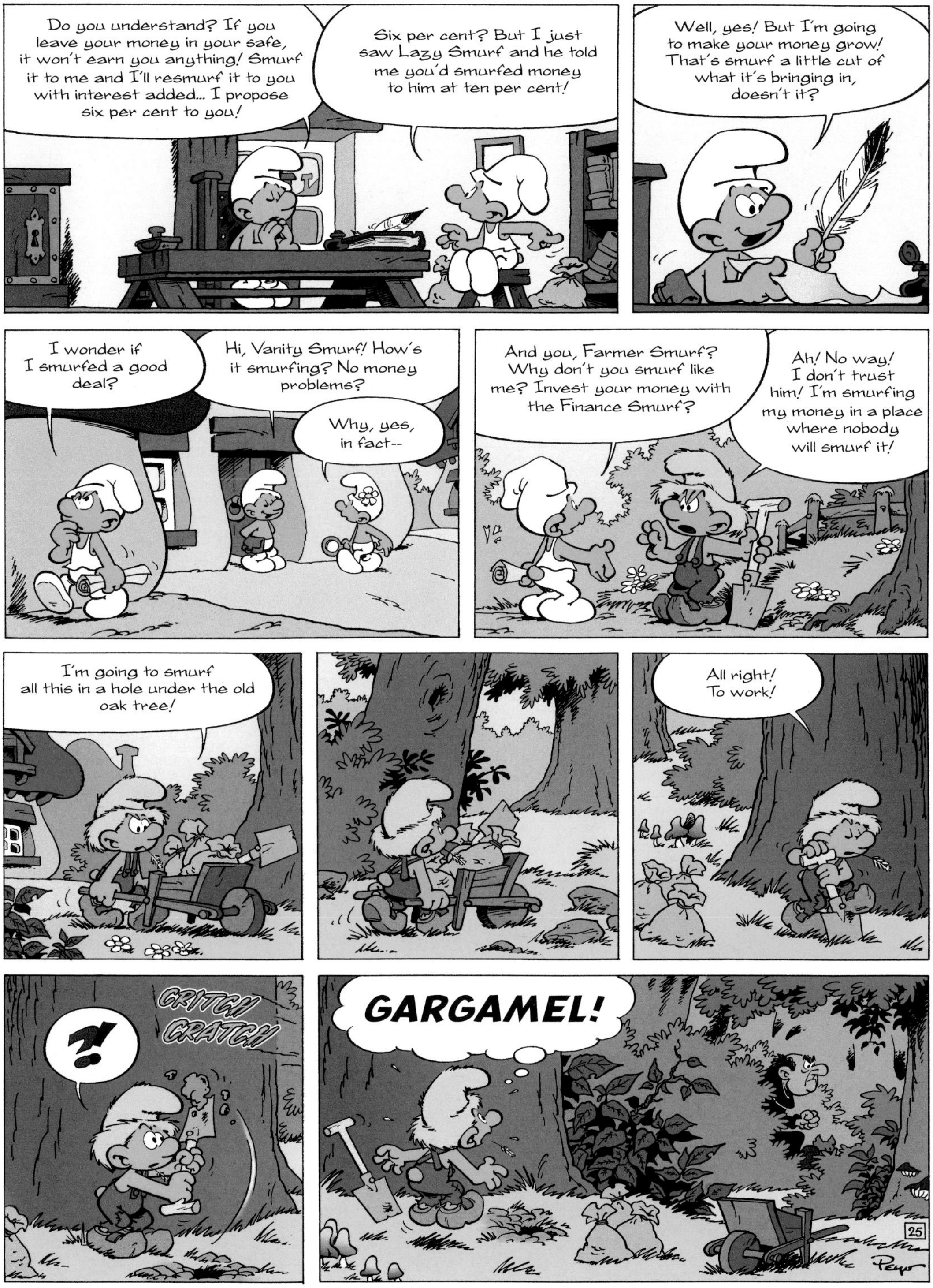

Do you understand? If you leave your money in your safe, it won't earn you anything! Smurf it to me and I'll resmurf it to you with interest added... I propose six per cent to you!
Six per cent? But I just saw Lazy Smurf and he told me you'd smurfed money to him at ten per cent!
Well, yes! But I'm going to make your money grow! That's smurf a little cut of what it's bringing in, doesn't it?
I wonder if I smurfed a good deal?
Hi, Vanity Smurf! How's it smurfing? No money problems?
Why, yes, in fact--
And you, Farmer Smurf? Why don't you smurf like me? Invest your money with the Finance Smurf?
Ah! No way! I don't trust him! I'm smurfing my money in a place where nobody will smurf it!
I'm going to smurf all this in a hole under the old oak tree!
All right! To work!
CRITCH CRATCH
?!
GARGAMEL!
25
Peyo

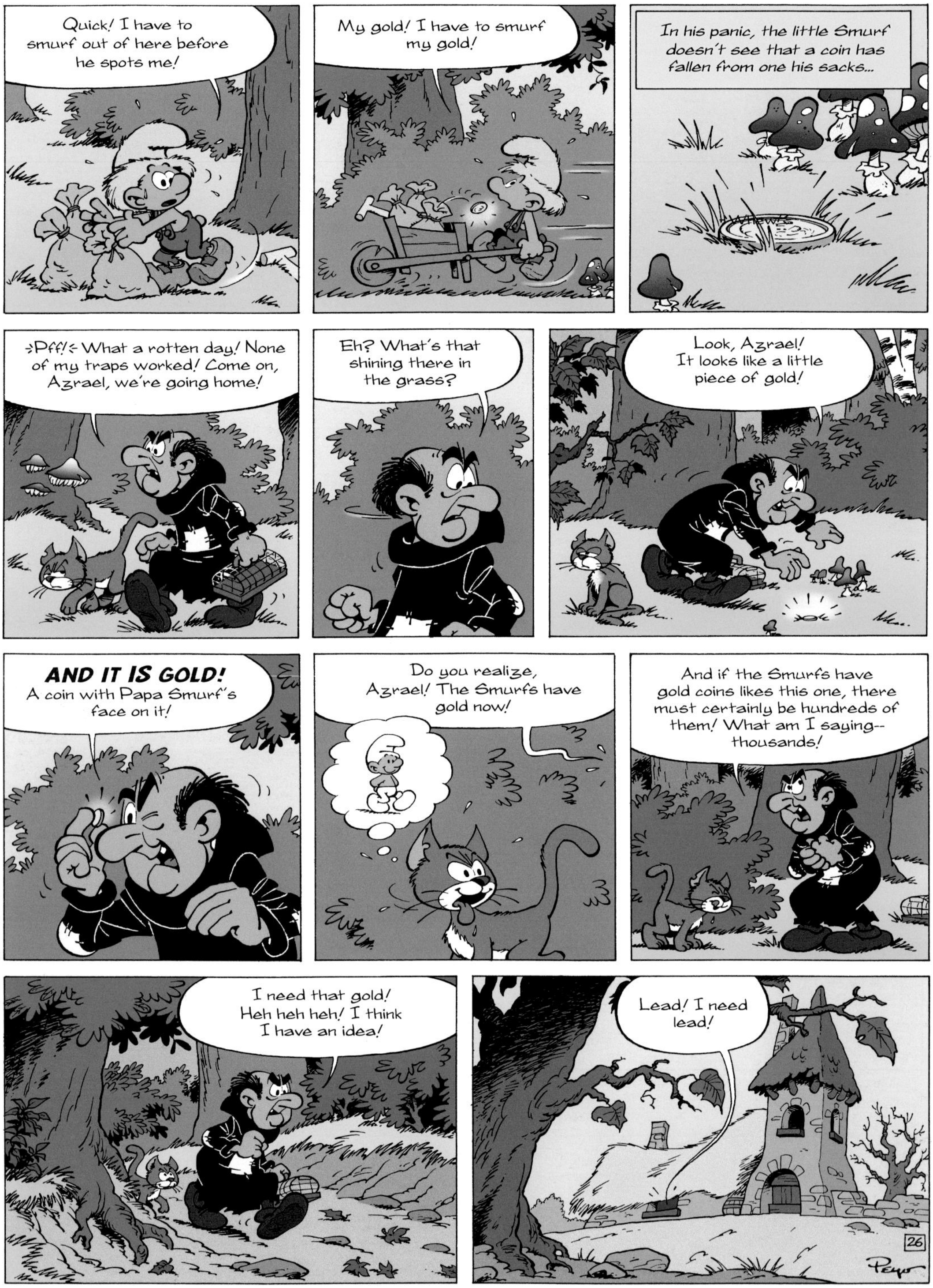
Quick! I have to smurf out of here before he spots me!
My gold! I have to smurf my gold!
In his panic, the little Smurf doesn't see that a coin has fallen from one his sacks...
>Pff!< What a rotten day! None of my traps worked! Come on, Azrael, we're going home!
Eh? What's that shining there in the grass?
Look, Azrael! It looks like a little piece of gold!
AND IT IS GOLD!
A coin with Papa Smurf's face on it!
Do you realize, Azrael! The Smurfs have gold now!
And if the Smurfs have gold coins likes this one, there must certainly be hundreds of them! What am I saying-- thousands!
I need that gold! Heh heh heh! I think I have an idea!
Lead! I need lead!
26
Peyo

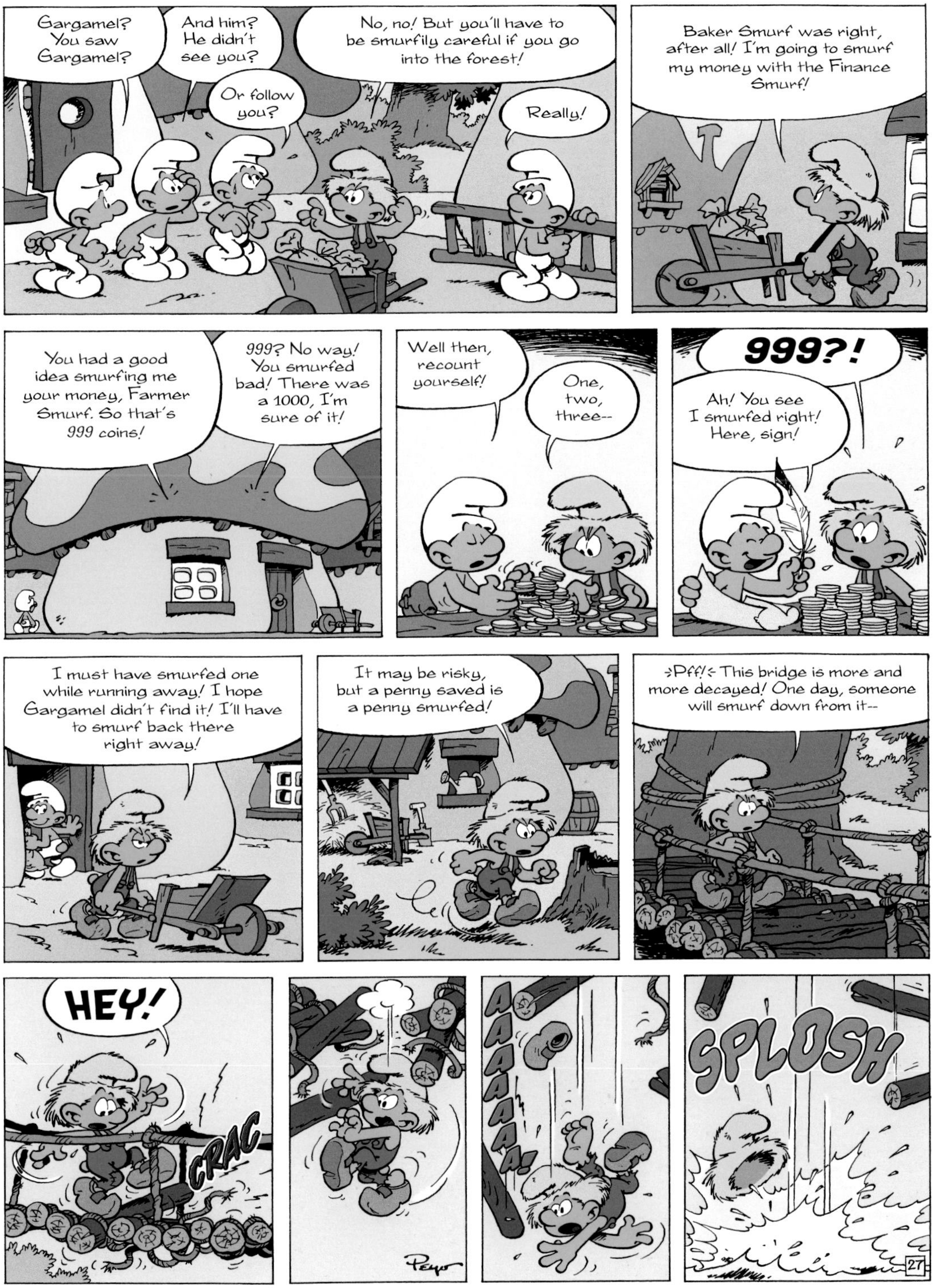
Gargamel? You saw Gargamel?
And him? He didn't see you?
Or follow you?
No, no! But you'll have to be smurfily careful if you go into the forest!
Really!
Baker Smurf was right, after all! I'm going to smurf my money with the Finance Smurf!
You had a good idea smurfing me your money, Farmer Smurf. So that's 999 coins!
999? No way! You smurfed bad! There was a 1000, I'm sure of it!
Well then, recount yourself!
One, two, three--
999?!
Ah! You see I smurfed right! Here, sign!
I must have smurfed one while running away! I hope Gargamel didn't find it! I'll have to smurf back there right away!
It may be risky, but a penny saved is a penny smurfed!
:Pff!: This bridge is more and more decayed! One day, someone will smurf down from it--
HEY!
CRAC
AAAAAAA!
SPLOSH
27

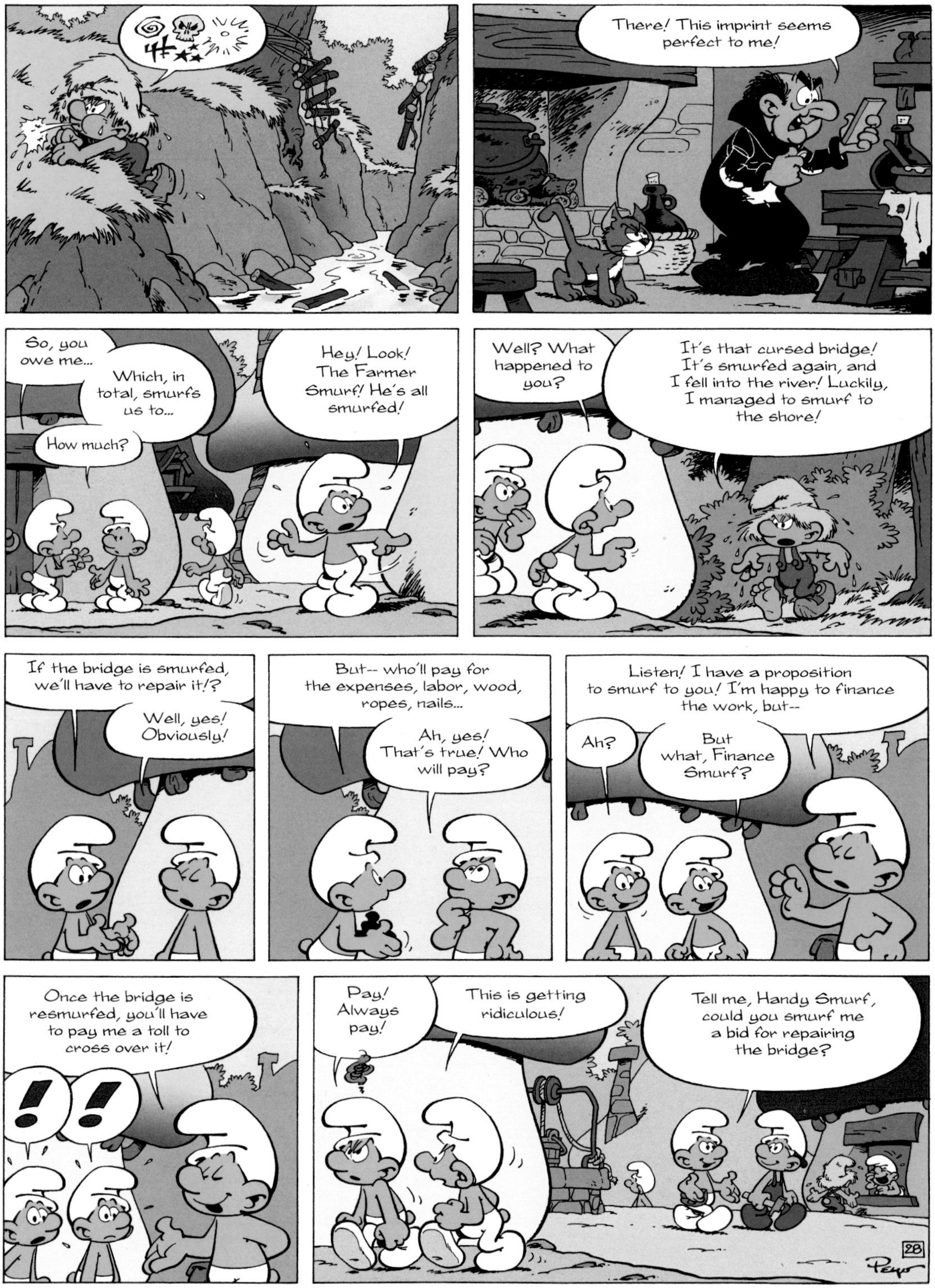
There! This imprint seems perfect to me!
So, you owe me...
Which, in total, smurfs us to...
How much?
Hey! Look! The Farmer Smurf! He's all smurfed!
Well? What happened to you?
It's that cursed bridge! It's smurfed again, and I fell into the river! Luckily, I managed to smurf to the shore!
If the bridge is smurfed, we'll have to repair it!?
Well, yes! Obviously!
But-- who'll pay for the expenses, labor, wood, ropes, nails...
Ah, yes! That's true! Who will pay?
Listen! I have a proposition to smurf to you! I'm happy to finance the work, but--
Ah?
But what, Finance Smurf?
Once the bridge is resmurfed, you'll have to pay me a toll to cross over it!
Pay! Always pay!
This is getting ridiculous!
Tell me, Handy Smurf, could you smurf me a bid for repairing the bridge?
28
Peyo

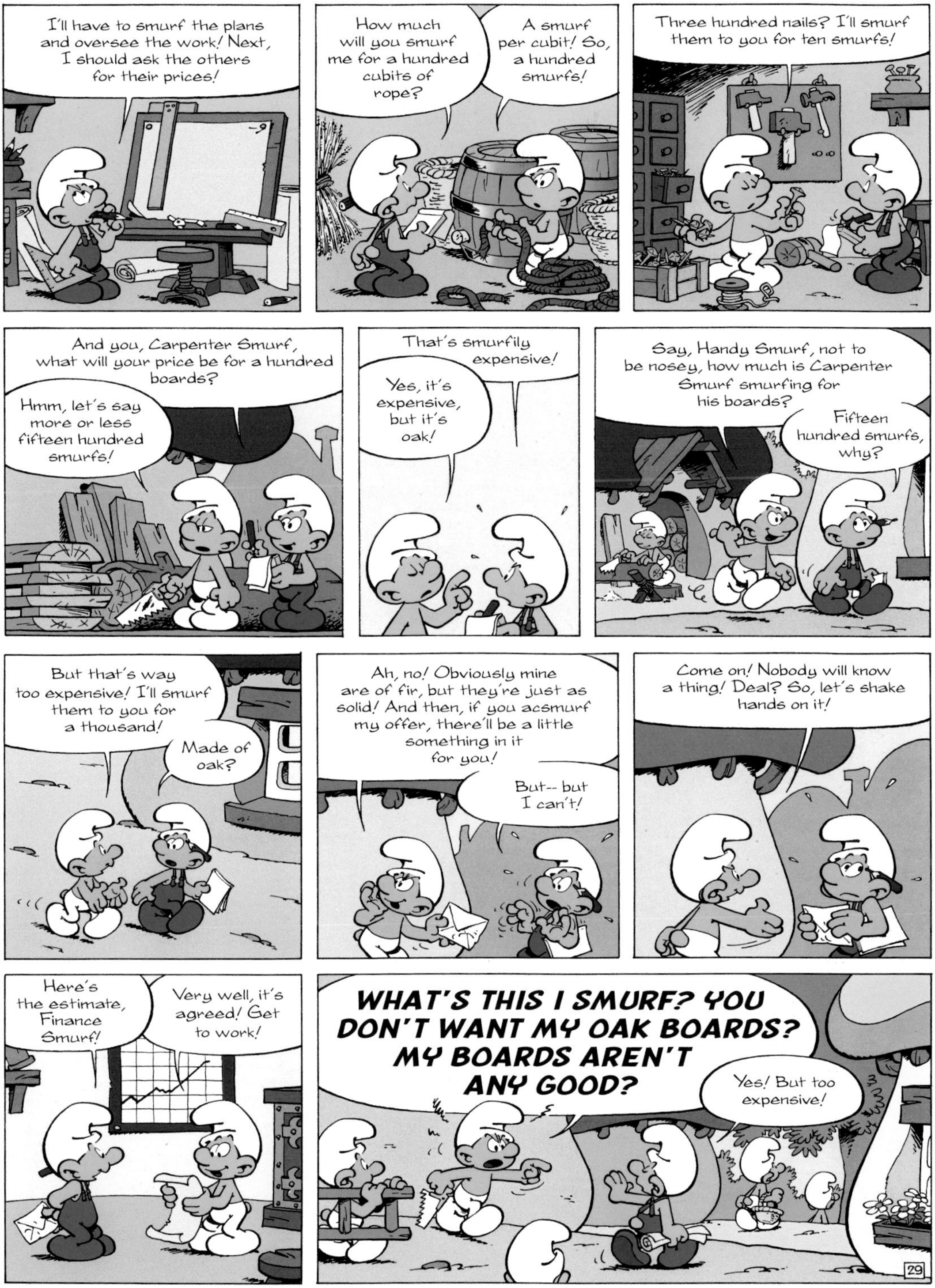
I'll have to smurf the plans and oversee the work! Next, I should ask the others for their prices!
How much will you smurf me for a hundred cubits of rope?
A smurf per cubit! So, a hundred smurfs!
Three hundred nails? I'll smurf them to you for ten smurfs!
And you, Carpenter Smurf, what will your price be for a hundred boards?
Hmm, let's say more or less fifteen hundred smurfs!
That's smurfily expensive!
Yes, it's expensive, but it's oak!
Say, Handy Smurf, not to be nosey, how much is Carpenter Smurf smurfing for his boards?
Fifteen hundred smurfs, why?
But that's way too expensive! I'll smurf them to you for a thousand!
Made of oak?
Ah, no! Obviously mine are of fir, but they're just as solid! And then, if you acsmurf my offer, there'll be a little something in it for you!
But-- but I can't!
Come on! Nobody will know a thing! Deal? So, let's shake hands on it!
Here's the estimate, Finance Smurf!
Very well, it's agreed! Get to work!
WHAT'S THIS I SMURF? YOU DON'T WANT MY OAK BOARDS? MY BOARDS AREN'T ANY GOOD?
Yes! But too expensive!
29

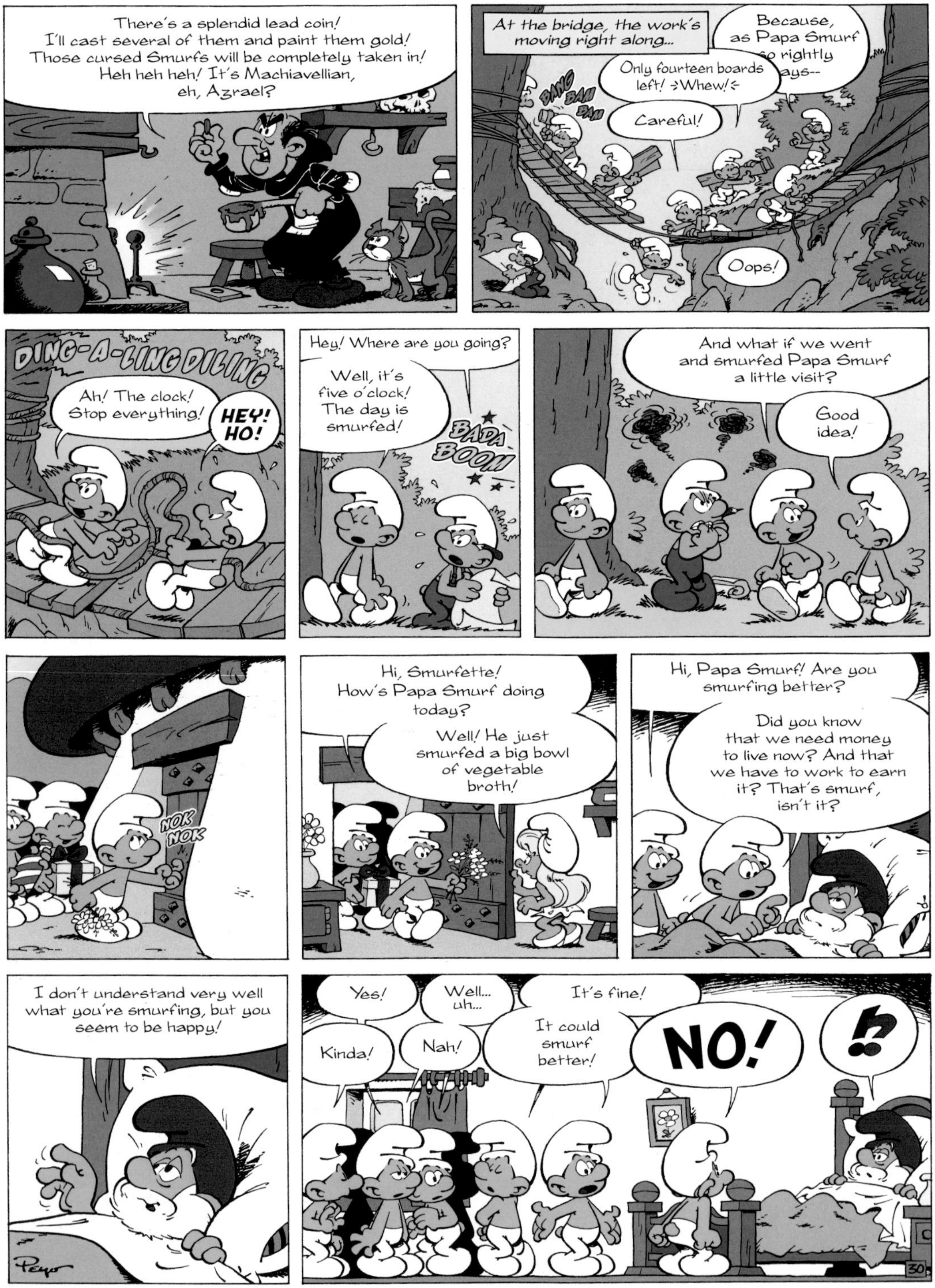
There's a splendid lead coin! I'll cast several of them and paint them gold! Those cursed Smurfs will be completely taken in! Heh heh heh! It's Machiavellian, eh, Azrael?
At the bridge, the work's moving right along...
BANG BAM BAM
Only fourteen boards left! Whew!
Careful!
Because, as Papa Smurf so rightly says--
Oops!
DING-A-LING DILING
Ah! The clock! Stop everything!
HEY! HO!
Hey! Where are you going?
Well, it's five o'clock! The day is smurfed!
BADA BOOM
And what if we went and smurfed Papa Smurf a little visit?
Good idea!
NOK NOK
Hi, Smurfette! How's Papa Smurf doing today?
Well! He just smurfed a big bowl of vegetable broth!
Hi, Papa Smurf! Are you smurfing better?
Did you know that we need money to live now? And that we have to work to earn it? That's smurf, isn't it?
I don't understand very well what you're smurfing, but you seem to be happy!
Yes!
Well... uh...
It's fine!
Kinda!
Nah!
It could smurf better!
NO!
!?
30

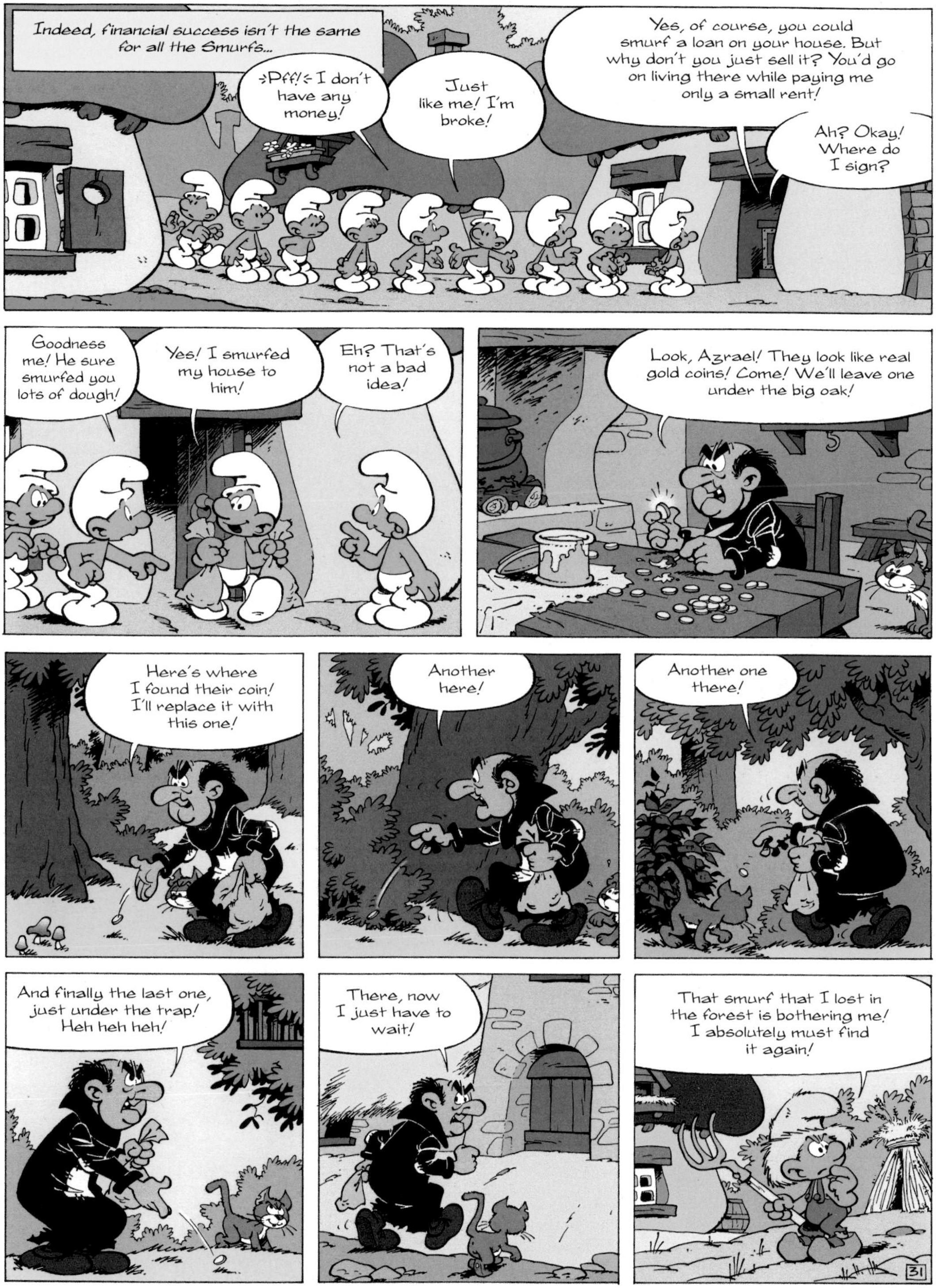

Indeed, financial success isn't the same for all the Smurfs...
Pff! I don't have any money!
Just like me! I'm broke!
Yes, of course, you could smurf a loan on your house. But why don't you just sell it? You'd go on living there while paying me only a small rent!
Ah? Okay! Where do I sign?
Goodness me! He sure smurfed you lots of dough!
Yes! I smurfed my house to him!
Eh? That's not a bad idea!
Look, Azrael! They look like real gold coins! Come! We'll leave one under the big oak!
Here's where I found their coin! I'll replace it with this one!
Another here!
Another one there!
And finally the last one, just under the trap! Heh heh heh!
There, now I just have to wait!
That smurf that I lost in the forest is bothering me! I absolutely must find it again!
31

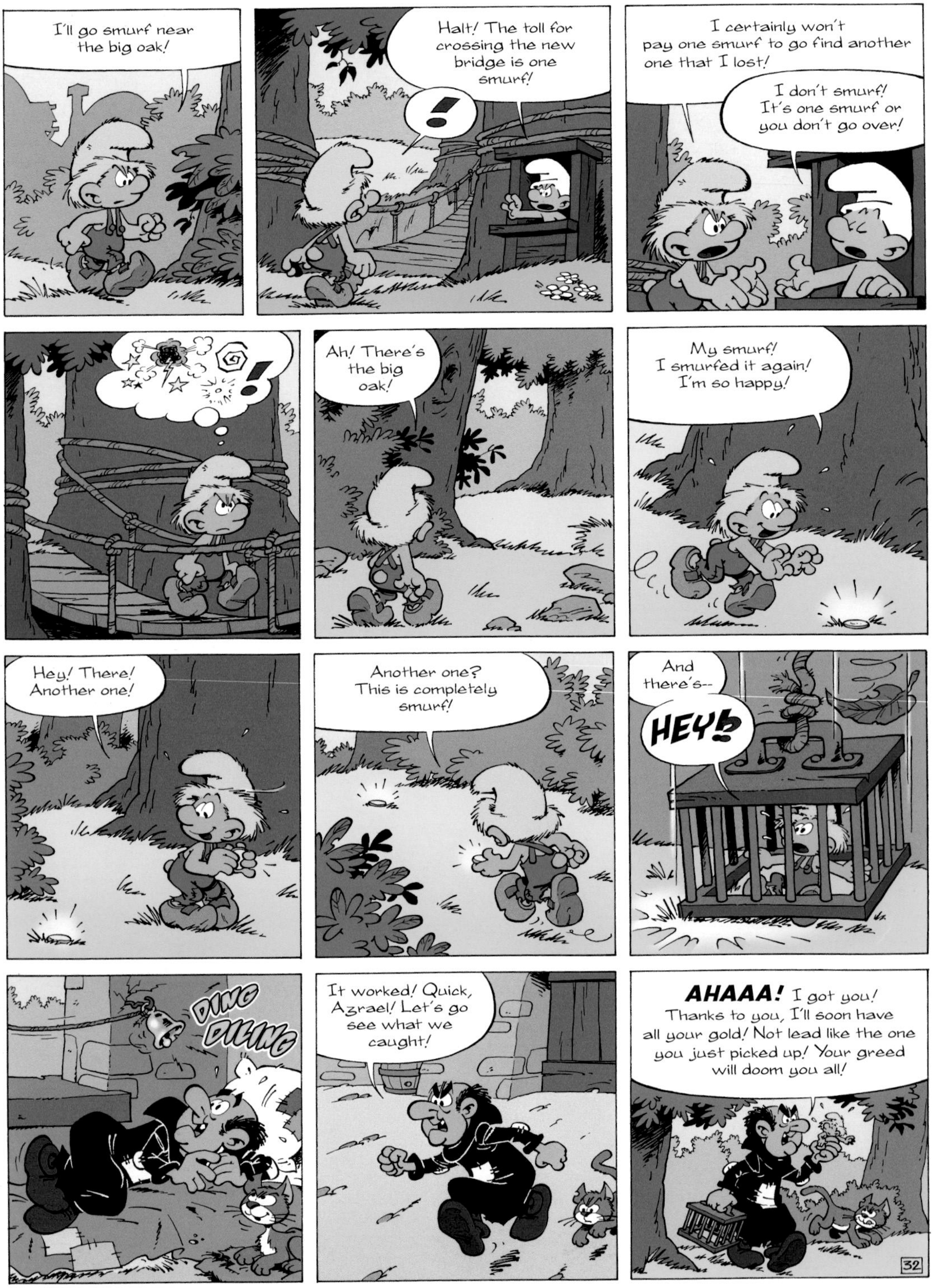
I'll go smurf near the big oak!
Halt! The toll for crossing the new bridge is one smurf!
!
I certainly won't pay one smurf to go find another one that I lost!
I don't smurf! It's one smurf or you don't go over!
!
Ah! There's the big oak!
My smurf! I smurfed it again! I'm so happy!
Hey! There! Another one!
Another one? This is completely smurf!
And there's--
HEY!?
DING DILING
It worked! Quick, Azrael! Let's go see what we caught!
AHAAA! I got you! Thanks to you, I'll soon have all your gold! Not lead like the one you just picked up! Your greed will doom you all!
32

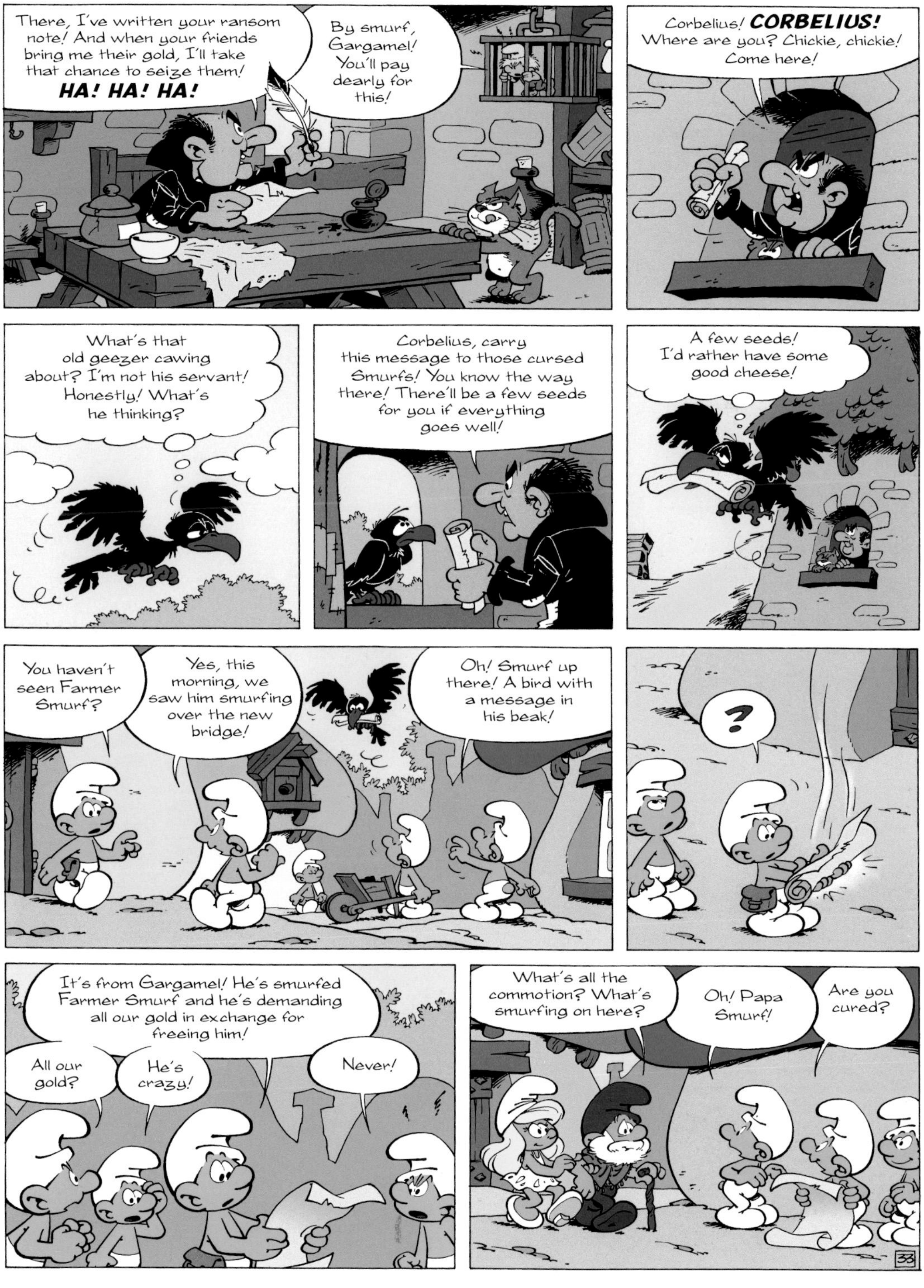
There, I've written your ransom note! And when your friends bring me their gold, I'll take that chance to seize them! HA! HA! HA!
By smurf, Gargamel! You'll pay dearly for this!
Corbelius! CORBELIUS! Where are you? Chickie, chickie! Come here!
What's that old geezer cawing about? I'm not his servant! Honestly! What's he thinking?
Corbelius, carry this message to those cursed Smurfs! You know the way there! There'll be a few seeds for you if everything goes well!
A few seeds! I'd rather have some good cheese!
You haven't seen Farmer Smurf?
Yes, this morning, we saw him smurfing over the new bridge!
Oh! Smurf up there! A bird with a message in his beak!
?
It's from Gargamel! He's smurfed Farmer Smurf and he's demanding all our gold in exchange for freeing him!
All our gold?
He's crazy!
Never!
What's all the commotion? What's smurfing on here?
Oh! Papa Smurf!
Are you cured?

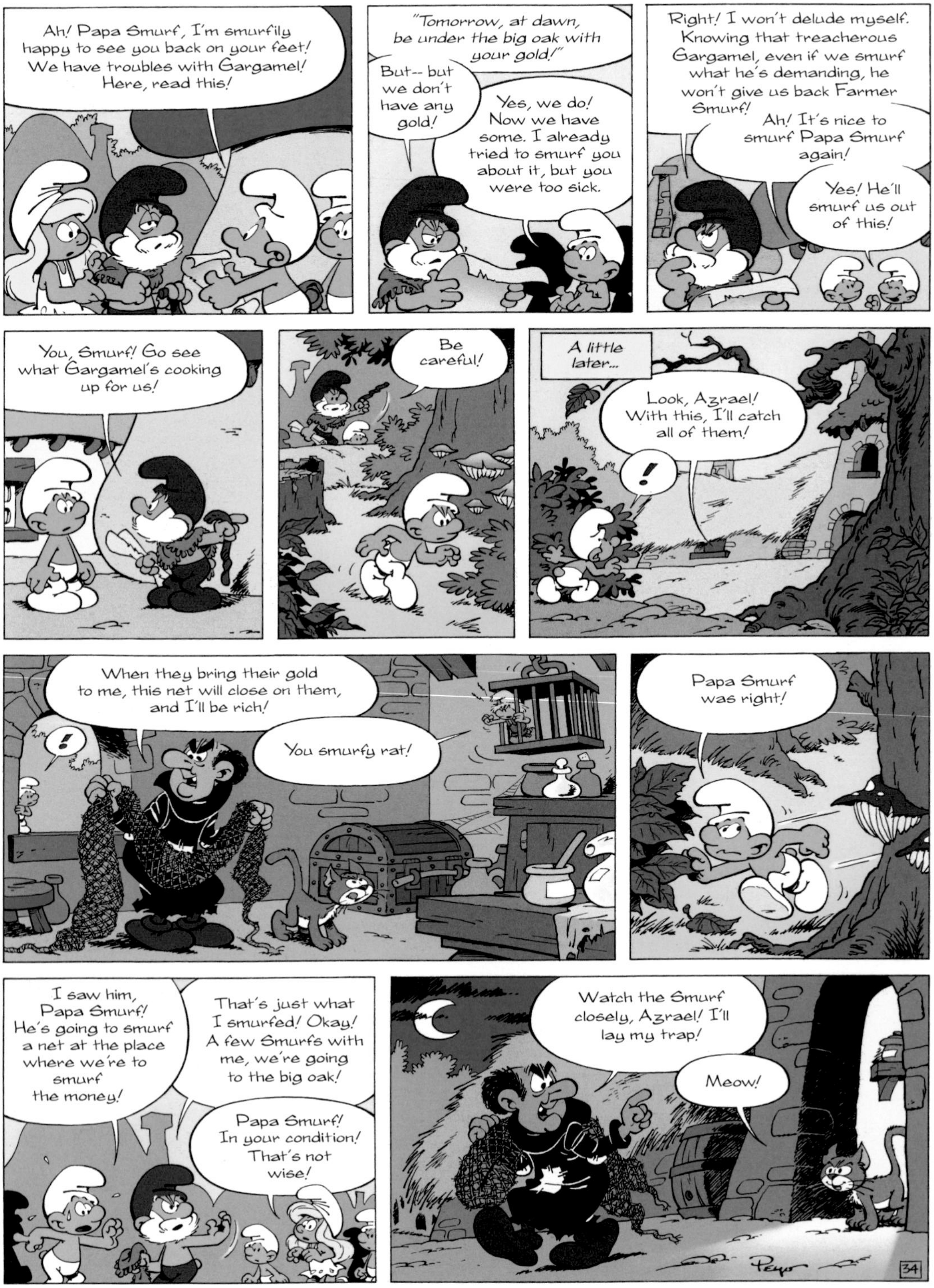
Ah! Papa Smurf, I'm smurfily happy to see you back on your feet! We have troubles with Gargamel! Here, read this!
"Tomorrow, at dawn, be under the big oak with your gold!"
But-- but we don't have any gold!
Yes, we do! Now we have some. I already tried to smurf you about it, but you were too sick.
Right! I won't delude myself. Knowing that treacherous Gargamel, even if we smurf what he's demanding, he won't give us back Farmer Smurf!
Ah! It's nice to smurf Papa Smurf again!
Yes! He'll smurf us out of this!
You, Smurf! Go see what Gargamel's cooking up for us!
Be careful!
A little later...
Look, Azrael! With this, I'll catch all of them!
!
When they bring their gold to me, this net will close on them, and I'll be rich!
!
You smurfy rat!
Papa Smurf was right!
I saw him, Papa Smurf! He's going to smurf a net at the place where we're to smurf the money!
That's just what I smurfed! Okay! A few Smurfs with me, we're going to the big oak!
Papa Smurf! In your condition! That's not wise!
Watch the Smurf closely, Azrael! I'll lay my trap!
Meow!
Peyo
34

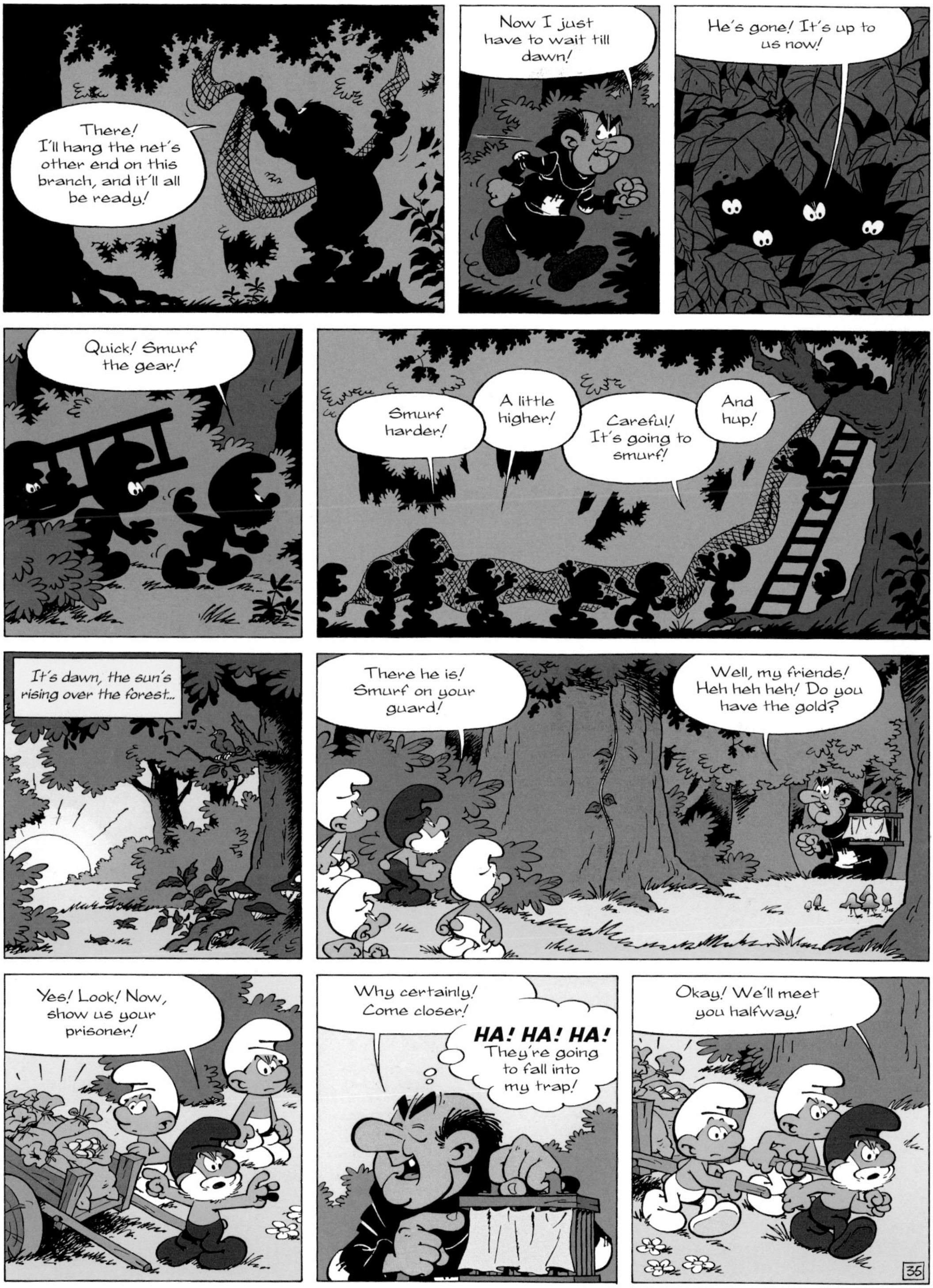
There! I'll hang the net's other end on this branch, and it'll all be ready!
Now I just have to wait till dawn!
He's gone! It's up to us now!
Quick! Smurf the gear!
Smurf harder!
A little higher!
Careful! It's going to smurf!
And hup!
It's dawn, the sun's rising over the forest...
There he is! Smurf on your guard!
Well, my friends! Heh heh heh! Do you have the gold?
Yes! Look! Now, show us your prisoner!
Why certainly! Come closer!
HA! HA! HA! They're going to fall into my trap!
Okay! We'll meet you halfway!
35

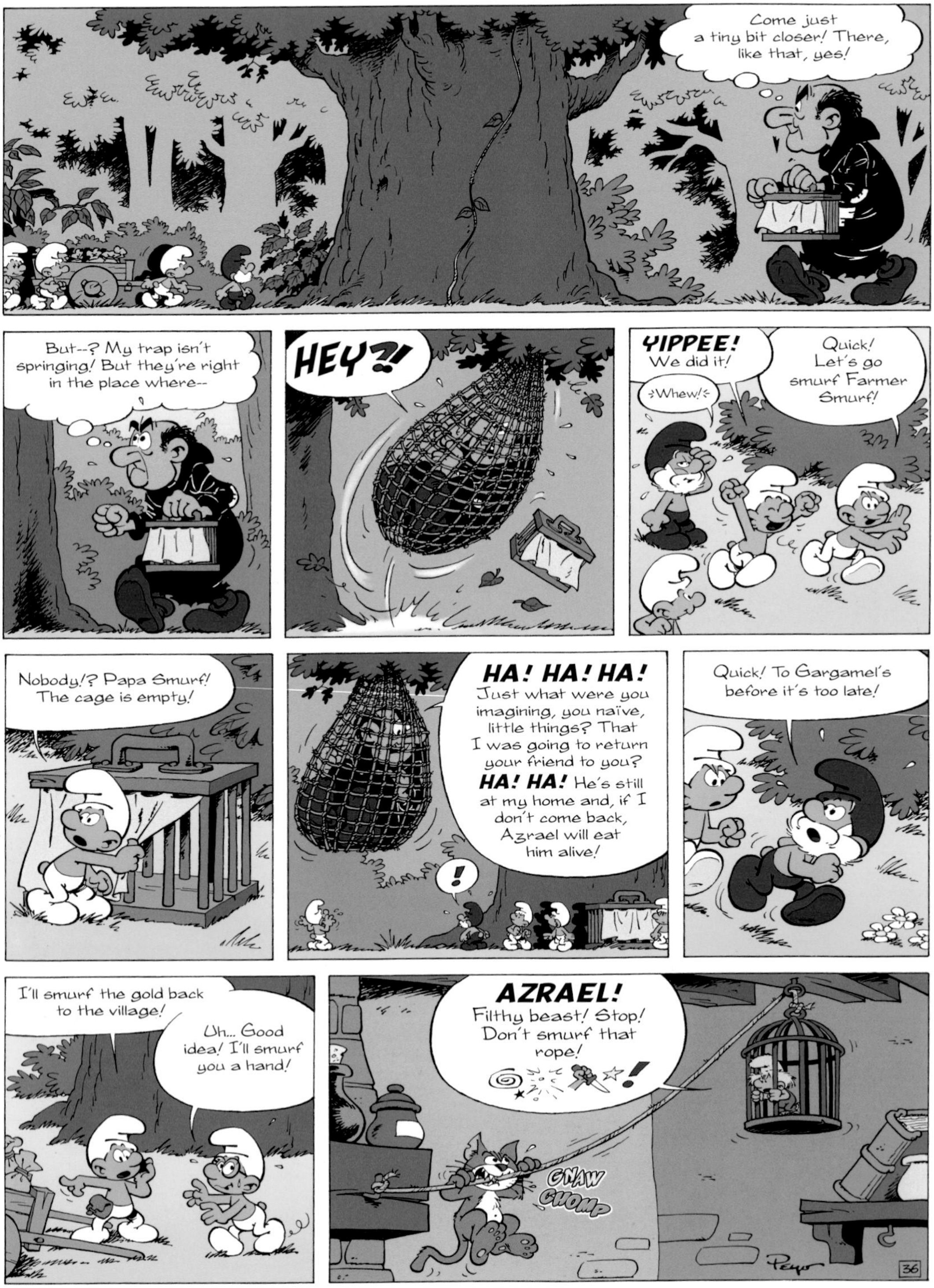
Come just a tiny bit closer! There, like that, yes!
But--? My trap isn't springing! But they're right in the place where--
HEY?!
YIPPEE! We did it!
Whew!
Quick! Let's go smurf Farmer Smurf!
Nobody!? Papa Smurf! The cage is empty!
HA! HA! HA! Just what were you imagining, you naïve, little things? That I was going to return your friend to you? HA! HA! He's still at my home and, if I don't come back, Azrael will eat him alive!
!
Quick! To Gargamel's before it's too late!
I'll smurf the gold back to the village!
Uh... Good idea! I'll smurf you a hand!
AZRAEL! Filthy beast! Stop! Don't smurf that rope!
GNAW CHOMP
Peyo
36

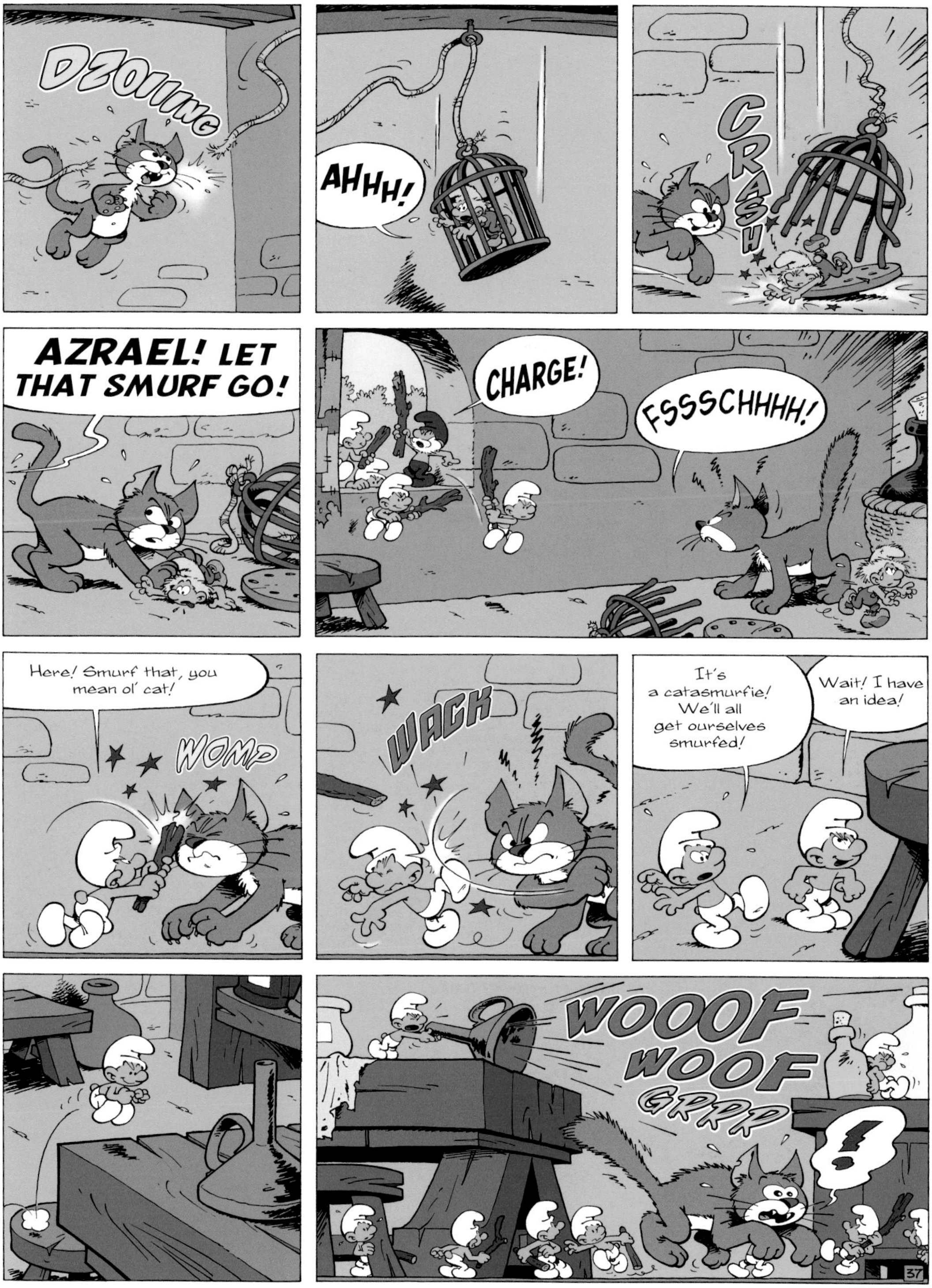
DZOIIING
AHHH!
CRASH
AZRAEL! LET THAT SMURF GO!
CHARGE!
FSSSCHHHH!
Here! Smurf that, you mean ol' cat!
WOMP
WACK
It's a catasmurfie! We'll all get ourselves smurfed!
Wait! I have an idea!
WOOOF
WOOOF
GRRR
!
37

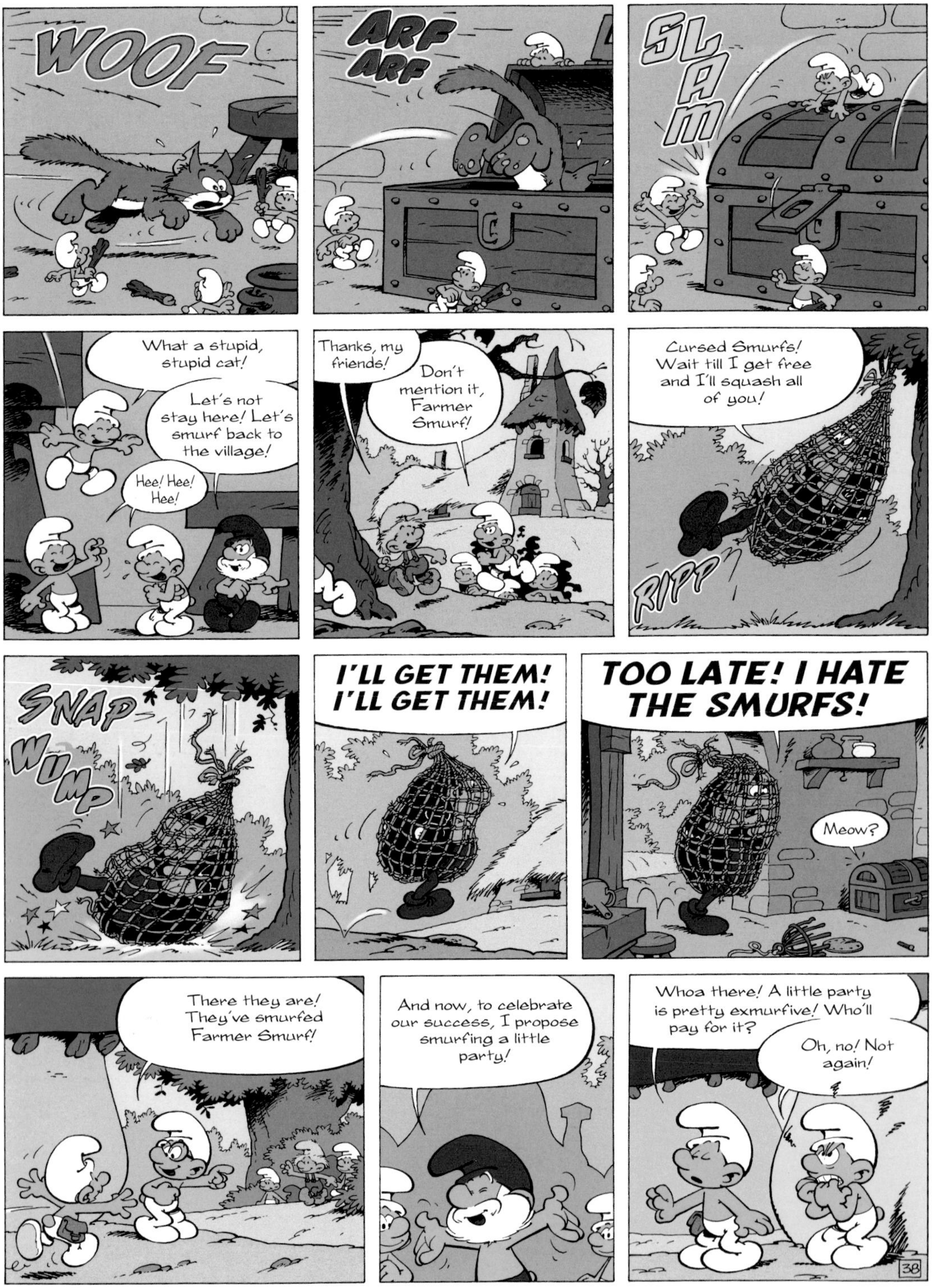
WOOF
ARF ARF
SLAM
What a stupid, stupid cat!
Let's not stay here! Let's smurf back to the village!
Hee! Hee! Hee!
Thanks, my friends!
Don't mention it, Farmer Smurf!
Cursed Smurfs! Wait till I get free and I'll squash all of you!
RIPP
SNAP
WUMP
I'LL GET THEM! I'LL GET THEM!
TOO LATE! I HATE THE SMURFS!
Meow?
There they are! They've smurfed Farmer Smurf!
And now, to celebrate our success, I propose smurfing a little party!
Whoa there! A little party is pretty exmurfive! Who'll pay for it?
Oh, no! Not again!
38

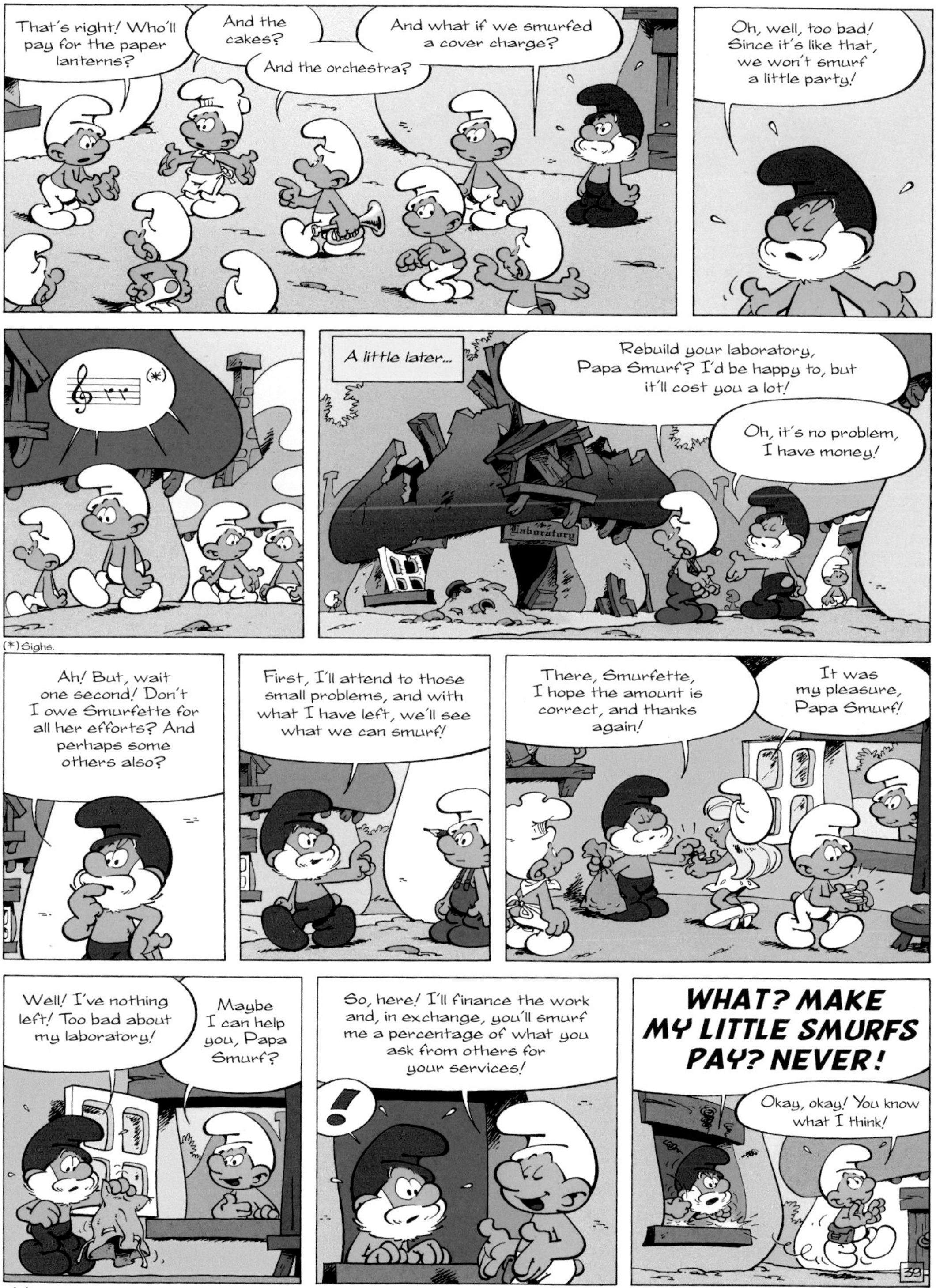
That's right! Who'll pay for the paper lanterns?
And the cakes?
And the orchestra?
And what if we smurfed a cover charge?
Oh, well, too bad! Since it's like that, we won't smurf a little party!
(*)
A little later...
Rebuild your laboratory, Papa Smurf? I'd be happy to, but it'll cost you a lot!
Oh, it's no problem, I have money!
Laboratory
Ah! But, wait one second! Don't I owe Smurfette for all her efforts? And perhaps some others also?
First, I'll attend to those small problems, and with what I have left, we'll see what we can smurf!
There, Smurfette, I hope the amount is correct, and thanks again!
It was my pleasure, Papa Smurf!
Well! I've nothing left! Too bad about my laboratory!
Maybe I can help you, Papa Smurf?
So, here! I'll finance the work and, in exchange, you'll smurf me a percentage of what you ask from others for your services!
!
WHAT? MAKE MY LITTLE SMURFS PAY? NEVER!
Okay, okay! You know what I think!
39

(*) Sighs.

(*)

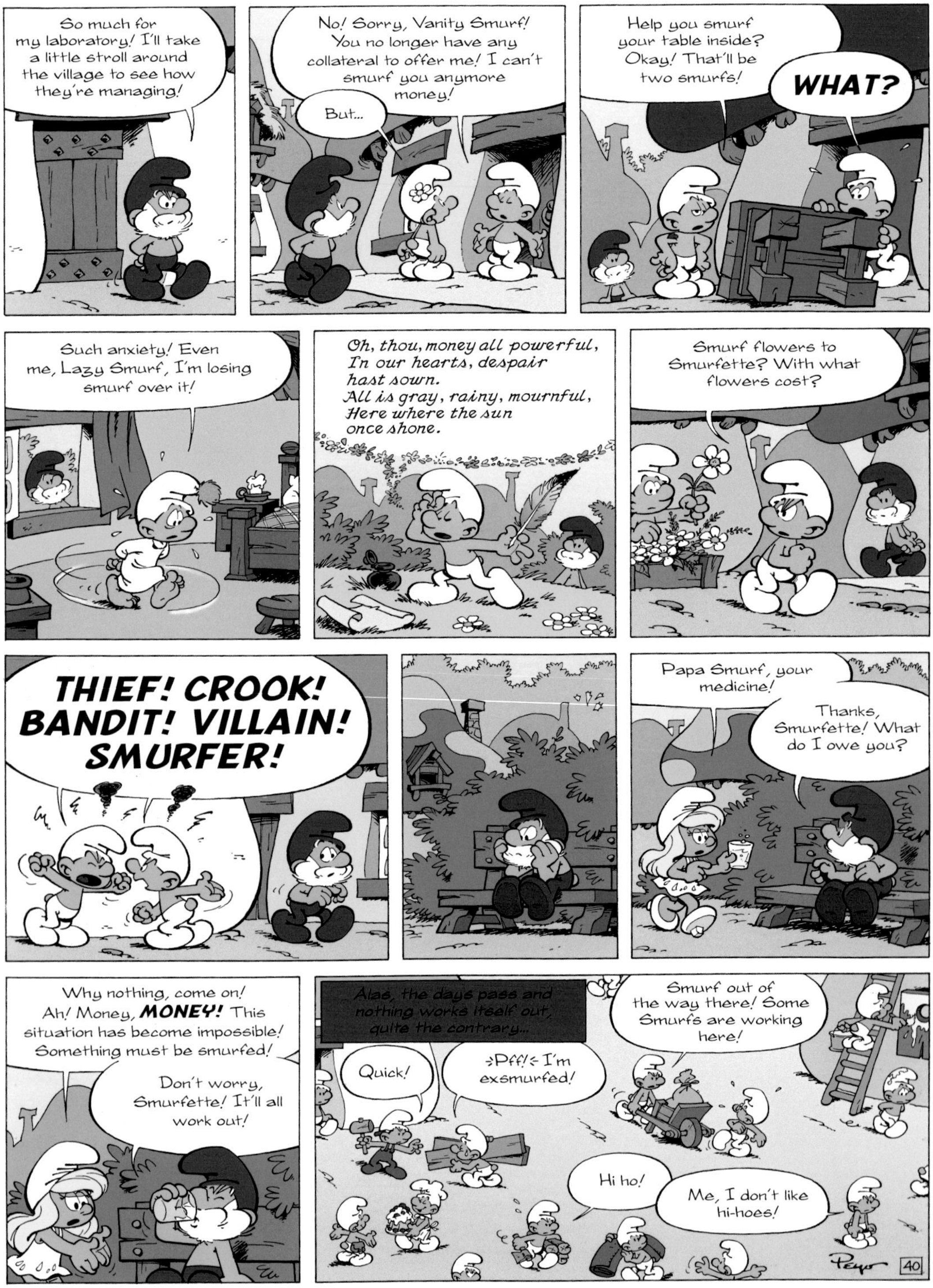
So much for my laboratory! I'll take a little stroll around the village to see how they're managing!
No! Sorry, Vanity Smurf! You no longer have any collateral to offer me! I can't smurf you anymore money!
But...
Help you smurf your table inside? Okay! That'll be two smurfs!
WHAT?
Such anxiety! Even me, Lazy Smurf, I'm losing smurf over it!
Oh, thou, money all powerful,
In our hearts, despair
hast sown.
All is gray, rainy, mournful,
Here where the sun
once shone.
Smurf flowers to Smurfette? With what flowers cost?
THIEF! CROOK! BANDIT! VILLAIN! SMURFER!
Papa Smurf, your medicine!
Thanks, Smurfette! What do I owe you?
Why nothing, come on! Ah! Money, MONEY! This situation has become impossible! Something must be smurfed!
Don't worry, Smurfette! It'll all work out!
Alas, the days pass and nothing works itself out, quite the contrary...
Quick!
Pff! I'm exsmurfed!
Smurf out of the way there! Some Smurfs are working here!
Hi ho!
Me, I don't like hi-hoes!
Peyo
40

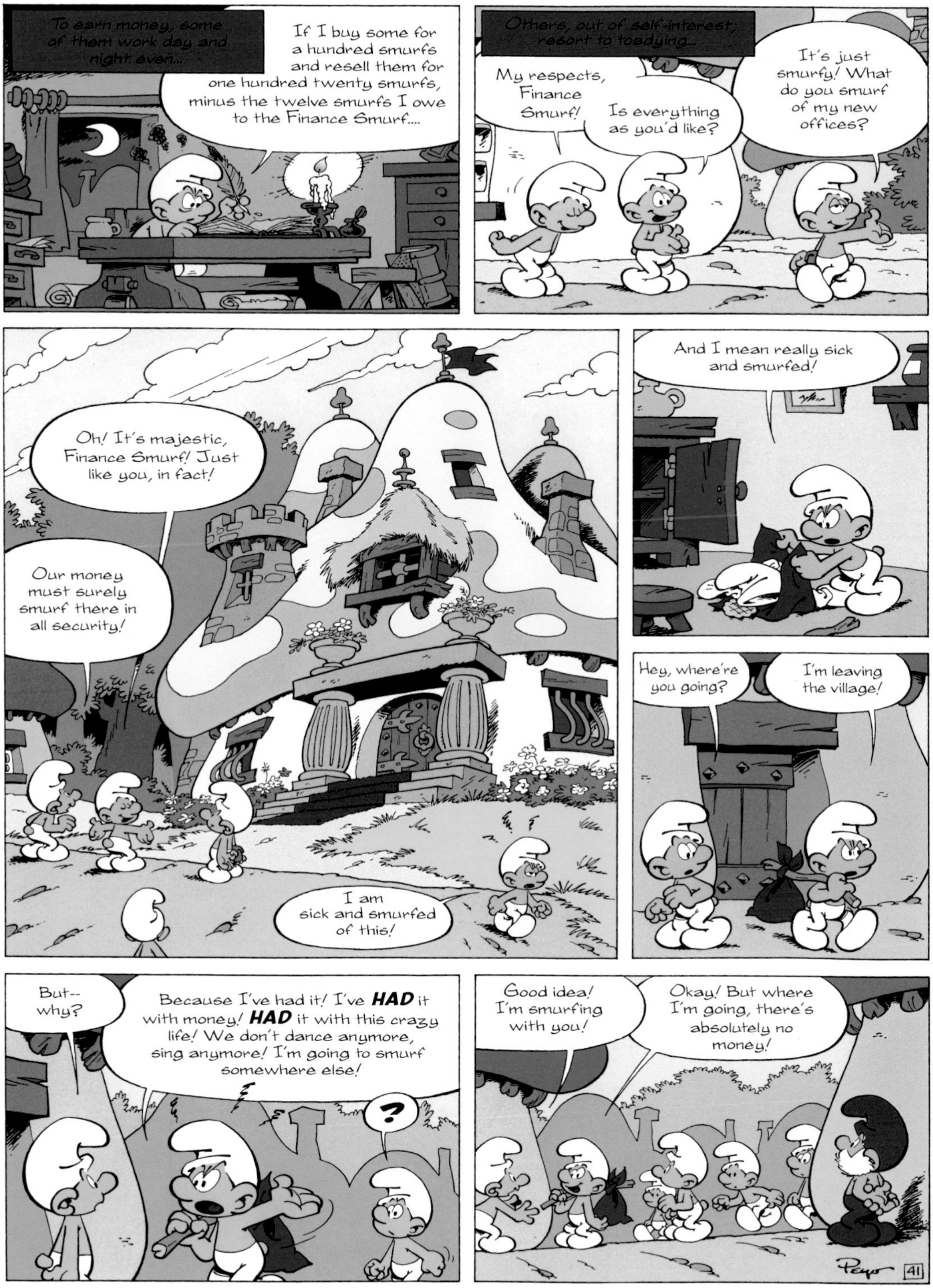
To earn money, some of them work day and night even...
If I buy some for a hundred smurfs and resell them for one hundred twenty smurfs, minus the twelve smurfs I owe to the Finance Smurf....
Others, out of self-interest, resort to toadying...
My respects, Finance Smurf!
Is everything as you'd like?
It's just smurfy! What do you smurf of my new offices?
Oh! It's majestic, Finance Smurf! Just like you, in fact!
Our money must surely smurf there in all security!
I am sick and smurfed of this!
And I mean really sick and smurfed!
Hey, where're you going?
I'm leaving the village!
But-- why?
Because I've had it! I've **HAD** it with money! **HAD** it with this crazy life! We don't dance anymore, sing anymore! I'm going to smurf somewhere else!
?
Good idea! I'm smurfing with you!
Okay! But where I'm going, there's absolutely no money!
Peyo
41

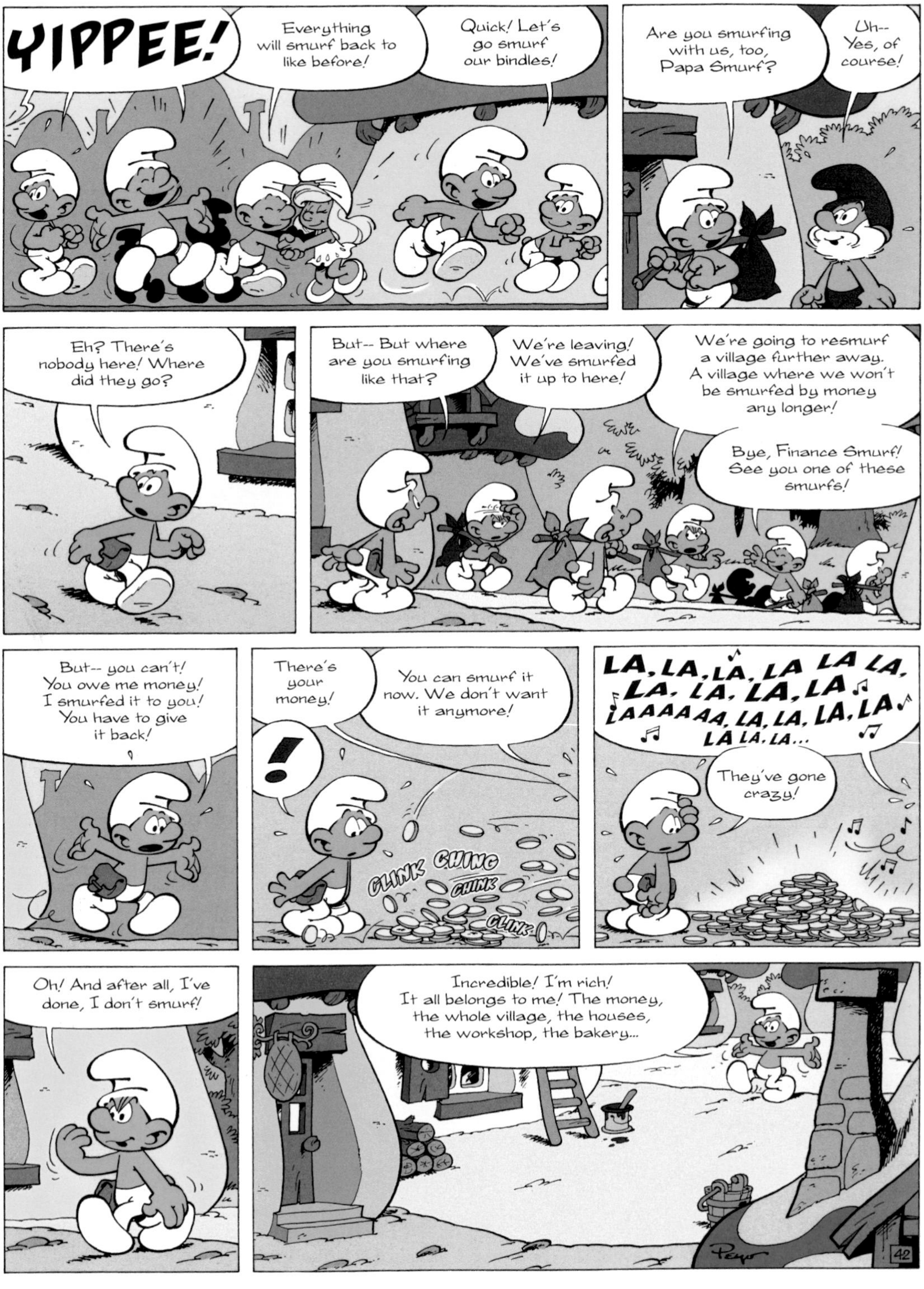
YIPPEE!
Everything will smurf back to like before!
Quick! Let's go smurf our bindles!
Are you smurfing with us, too, Papa Smurf?
Uh-- Yes, of course!
Eh? There's nobody here! Where did they go?
But-- But where are you smurfing like that?
We're leaving! We've smurfed it up to here!
We're going to resmurf a village further away. A village where we won't be smurfed by money any longer!
Bye, Finance Smurf! See you one of these smurfs!
But-- you can't! You owe me money! I smurfed it to you! You have to give it back!
There's your money!
You can smurf it now. We don't want it anymore!
!
CLINK CHING CHINK CLINK
LA, LA, LA, LA LA LA, LA, LA, LA, LA LAAAAAA, LA, LA, LA, LA LA LA, LA...
They've gone crazy!
Oh! And after all, I've done, I don't smurf!
Incredible! I'm rich! It all belongs to me! The money, the whole village, the houses, the workshop, the bakery...
Peyo
42

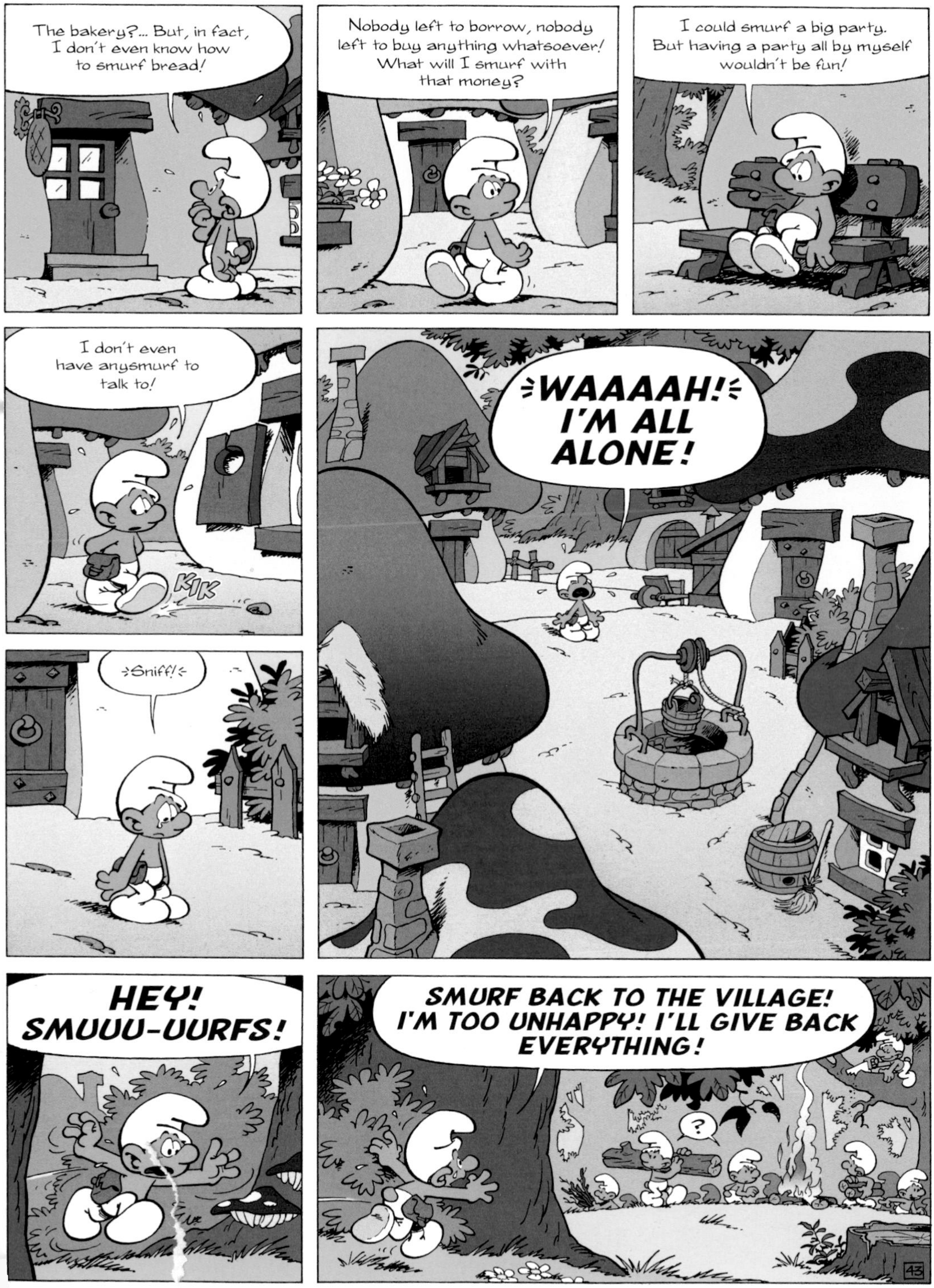
The bakery?... But, in fact, I don't even know how to smurf bread!
Nobody left to borrow, nobody left to buy anything whatsoever! What will I smurf with that money?
I could smurf a big party. But having a party all by myself wouldn't be fun!
I don't even have anysmurf to talk to!
KIK
WAAAAH! I'M ALL ALONE!
Sniff!
HEY! SMUUU-UURFS!
SMURF BACK TO THE VILLAGE! I'M TOO UNHAPPY! I'LL GIVE BACK EVERYTHING!
?
43

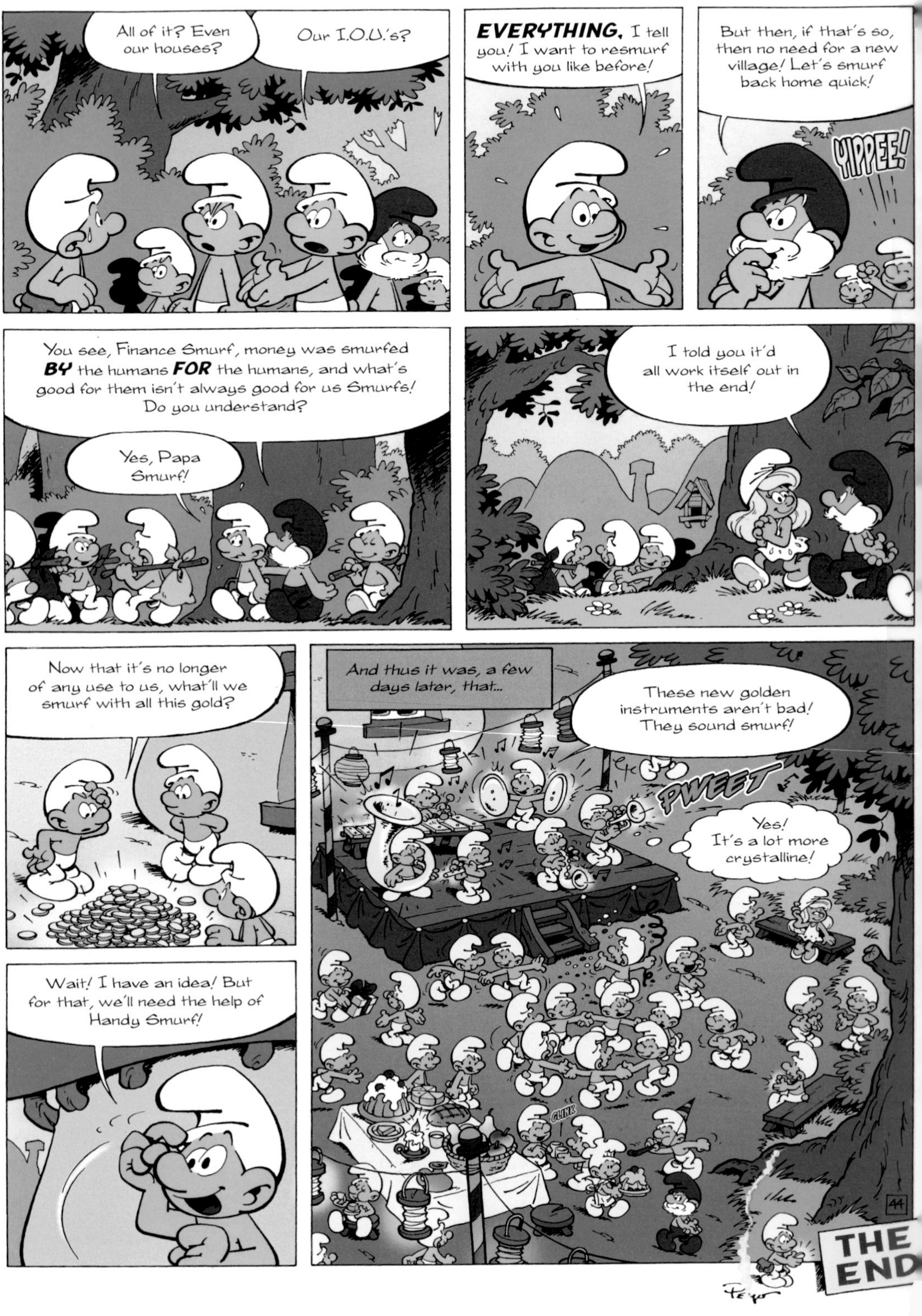
All of it? Even our houses?
Our I.O.U.'s?
EVERYTHING, I tell you! I want to resmurf with you like before!
But then, if that's so, then no need for a new village! Let's smurf back home quick!
YIPPEE!
You see, Finance Smurf, money was smurfed BY the humans FOR the humans, and what's good for them isn't always good for us Smurfs! Do you understand?
Yes, Papa Smurf!
I told you it'd all work itself out in the end!
Now that it's no longer of any use to us, what'll we smurf with all this gold?
Wait! I have an idea! But for that, we'll need the help of Handy Smurf!
And thus it was, a few days later, that...
These new golden instruments aren't bad! They sound smurf!
PWEET
Yes! It's a lot more crystalline!
CLINK
44
THE END
Peyo